DOCTOR WHO
AND THE
ABOMINABLE SNOWMEN

THE CHANGING FACE OF DOCTOR WHO
The cover illustration and others contained within this
book portray the second DOCTOR WHO whose physical
appearance was later altered by the Time Lords.

Also available from BBC Books:

DOCTOR WHO AND THE DALEKS
David Whitaker

DOCTOR WHO AND THE CRUSADERS
David Whitaker

DOCTOR WHO AND THE CYBERMEN
Gerry Davis

DOCTOR WHO AND THE AUTON INVASION
Terrance Dicks

DOCTOR WHO AND THE CAVE MONSTERS
Malcolm Hulke

DOCTOR WHO
AND THE
ABOMINABLE
SNOWMEN

Based on the BBC television serial *The Abominable Snowmen* by Mervyn Haisman and Henry Lincoln by arrangement with the BBC

TERRANCE DICKS

Introduction by
STEPHEN BAXTER

Illustrated by
Alan Willow

BOOKS

3 5 7 9 10 8 6 4 2

Published in 2011 by BBC Books, an imprint of Ebury Publishing
A Random House Group Company
First published in 1974 by Universal-Tandem Publishing Co., Ltd.

Novelisation copyright © Terrance Dicks 1974
Original script © Mervyn Haisman and Henry Lincoln 1967
Illustrations © Alan Willow 1974
Introduction © Stephen Baxter 2011
The Changing Face of Doctor Who and About the Authors © Justin Richards 2011
Between the Lines © Steve Tribe 2011

BBC, DOCTOR WHO and TARDIS (word marks, logos and devices) are trademarks
of the British Broadcasting Corporation and are used under licence.

All rights reserved. No part of this publication may be reproduced, stored in a
retrieval system, or transmitted in any form or by any means, electronic, mechanical,
photocopying, recording or otherwise, without the prior permission of the copyright
owner.

The Random House Group Limited Reg. No. 954009

Addresses for companies within the Random House Group can be found at
www.randomhouse.co.uk

A CIP catalogue record for this book is available from the British Library.

ISBN 978 1 849 90192 5

MIX
Paper from
responsible sources
FSC® C016897
FSC
www.fsc.org

The Random House Group Limited supports The Forest Stewardship Council
(FSC®), the leading international forest certification organisation. Our books
carrying the FSC label are printed on FSC® certified paper. FSC is the only
forest certification scheme endorsed by the leading environmental organisations,
including Greenpeace. Our paper procurement policy can be found at
www.randomhouse.co.uk/environment

Commissioning editor: Albert DePetrillo
Editorial manager: Nicholas Payne
Series consultant: Justin Richards
Project editor: Steve Tribe
Cover design: Lee Binding © Woodlands Books Ltd, 2011
Cover illustration: Chris Achilleos
Production: Rebecca Jones

Printed and bound by CPI Group (UK) Ltd, Croydon, CR0 4YY

To buy books by your favourite authors and register for offers,
visit www.randomhouse.co.uk

Contents

INTRODUCTION
BY
Stephen Baxter

This novel is based on the *Doctor Who* serial 'The Abominable Snowmen'. I was not quite 10 years old when this serial was first broadcast by the BBC from September 1967. All these years later, I can remember the family watching the programme together in our living room, and I recall vivid images and scenes from the show: in this case the brooding mountain-top monastery, the enigmatic monks, the mixture of strange monsters and alien high-tech, the unfolding mystery: 'That horrible creature … What was it?' 'I dinna ken, lassie. But it was verra strong. Did you see what it did to my sword?'

'Snowmen' was a highlight of the second season starring Patrick Troughton, the Second Doctor. Troughton has always remained my own favourite Doctor, thanks to his charismatic mix of physical comedy, kindliness, cheeky quick wits, and, when he needed it, a deep authority. But Troughton was blessed with some excellent scripts and cracking productions. 'Snowmen' was sandwiched between a Cyberman adventure and the debut of that eerie foe from Mars, the Ice Warriors.

It was (almost) enough for us fans to forgive the BBC for apparently killing off the Daleks at the end of the previous series... Of course, as the Doctor knows, you can never write off the Daleks.

Shot in August and September 1967, this story featured a lot of location work, with Snowdonia in Wales standing in for Tibet. Professor Travers was played by the real-life father of Deborah Watling, who played the Doctor's companion Victoria. Even before 'Snowmen' was screened, the production team were so pleased with it that they commissioned a sequel, 'The Web of Fear', shown later in the same season, which features the Yeti infesting the London Underground: 'London, in fact the whole of England, might be completely wiped out!'

In 1973, when Target Books, a new imprint publishing children's titles, got the chance to publish novelisations of the *Doctor Who* serials, a call to the production office at the BBC brought an enthusiastic response from Script Editor Terrance Dicks, who volunteered to write some of the books himself. The first serial to be novelised was Jon Pertwee's debut adventure 'Spearhead from Space' (published as *Doctor Who and the Auton Invasion* and reissued along with this novel). It was the first book of any kind Dicks had written.

And it was the start of a seventeen-year association between Target and Dicks, who went on to write an astounding sixty-four novelisations, including *Doctor Who and the Abominable Snowmen* and *Doctor Who and the Web of Fear*. He also wrote *Doctor Who* tie-in books, stage plays and audio plays, and later contributed original *Doctor Who* novels for Virgin Publishing and the BBC, in addition to writing his own original children's books.

Working on *Doctor Who* was clearly a labour of love for Dicks – as well as a steady source of income, always invaluable for a freelance writer. In a history of the Target books published in 2007, Dicks said that some of the scripts for the new era of the show had been 'written by people who grew up reading my *Who* novelisations at their mother's knee. Some of them have been kind enough to tell me so … It was nice to still be a small part of the legend.'

Dicks deserves to be remembered, for his work showed a great deal of skill. He rendered the television stories into clear, straightforward, compelling prose. The novelising writer had to work in seamless introductions to the show's premise for new readers, as well as background character sketches of the companions. Sometimes other changes were necessary. In 'Snowmen', the writers had used the names of figures from the real history of Buddhism. *Doctor Who*'s then producer, Barry Letts, suggested Dicks change these slightly to avoid any risk of offence.

Dicks always worked hard to make his novels a proper reflection of their sources in the TV serials. He was quoted in that Target history as saying, 'I see the task of the novelisation as reproducing the effect of watching the TV show in the reader's head. Sometimes, with no budgetary restrictions, you can even improve on it.'

When the first Target books were published in 1973, I was a little older than the intended readership – though I read a good few of the books anyhow. And with the passage of time these books assumed an unexpected importance. The disastrous wiping of tapes of archived 1960s *Doctor Who* episodes is well known. The Troughton era seems to have been particularly hard hit; only one episode of 'Snowmen' is known to exist (Episode 2), and one of 'The Web of Fear' (Episode 1). (You can view these and other relic episodes on the BBC DVD *Lost in Time*.)

Nowadays there are audio versions of some of the lost shows, and even animated recreations of some missing episodes. But for a very long time the *only* way to experience these much-loved but long-vanished serials was through the Target novelisations. Thus Terrance Dicks and the other Target writers performed a quite invaluable service in 'saving' these stories, not only for the benefit of the original viewers of the lost shows, but also for the subsequent generations of fans who never got the chance to see them even once.

So don't think of this book as just another novel. It's a slice of *Who* history. And as you turn the page – travel back in time, to September 1967. It's only a year since England's World Cup win. In the year of the Summer of Love, the Beatles and the Stones are at their peak. As a *Who* fan you're sure to be aware that *Captain Scarlet and the Mysterons* has just made its TV debut.

And now it's twenty-five past five on a Saturday

afternoon, the *Grandstand* teleprinter has finished clattering out the football scores, and you join Dad before the thick glass screen of the family telly. The familiar radiophonic theme tune hisses out of the set's tiny speaker... a rush of psychedelic effects in silvery black and white washes away to reveal the Second Doctor's smiling face... and we dissolve to a scene of a sputtering camp fire on a bleak Tibetan mountainside... a lonely figure, huddled in the dark... an eerie scream... a huge, looming figure... a familiar blue box materialising...

The adventure begins.

The Changing Face of Doctor Who

The Second Doctor

This *Doctor Who* novel features the second incarnation of the Doctor. After his first encounter with the Cybermen, the Doctor changed form. His old body was apparently worn out, and so he replaced it with a new, younger one. The scratchy, arrogant old man that had been the First Doctor was replaced with a younger and apparently far softer character. The First Doctor's cold, analytical abilities gave way to apparent bluster and a tendency to panic under pressure.

But with the Second Doctor more than any other, first impressions are misleading. The Doctor's apparent bluster and ineptitude masks a deeper, darker nature. But there are moments too when the Second Doctor's humanity also shines through. There is ultimately no doubt that his raison d'être is to fight the evil in the universe.

Jamie

James Robert McCrimmon is the son of Donald McCrimmon, and a piper like his father and his father's father. Coming from 1746, Jamie is simple and straightforward, but he is also intelligent and blessed with a good deal of common sense. Almost everything is new to him, and while he struggles to understand he also enjoys the experience. Jamie is also extremely brave, never one to shirk a fight or run away.

Ultimately, Jamie sees the Doctor as a friend as well as a mentor. While he relishes the chance to travel and learn and have adventures, he also believes that the Doctor really does need his help.

Victoria

Victoria is a reluctant adventurer. She travels with the Doctor through necessity rather than choice after her father was exterminated by the Daleks, leaving her stranded on Skaro. Until she was kidnapped by the Daleks, Victoria led a sheltered and unsophisticated life. But she is clever and intelligent.

Despite the fact that both tease her at every opportunity, Victoria cares deeply for the Doctor and Jamie. But while she enjoys her time in their company, she still misses her father. She remains forever an unwilling adventurer.

1

The Secret of the Snows

High on the Himalayan mountainside the little camp fire was burning low. Edward Travers shivered, and huddled deeper inside his sleeping-bag. He was drifting in and out of an uneasy slumber, fantasy and reality merging and blurring in his mind. In his dream, he was at the Royal Geographical Society, addressing a scornful and hostile audience.

'Gentlemen, I assure you – the body of evidence that has accumulated over the years is undeniable. The Abominable Snowman does exist.'

He heard again the hated voice of his old rival, Professor Walters. *'If you're as sure as that, my dear Travers, I suggest you go and look for the beast!'*

Once more Travers heard the scornful laughter that followed. He heard his own voice. *'Thank you for the suggestion, sir. Perhaps I will.'*

Travers twisted and muttered in his sleep. Scene followed scene in his mind, like a jerky, speeded-up old film: the desperate struggle to raise money for his expedition; the final, half-scornful agreement of a Fleet Street editor to back him; the long journey to India; the endless days of overland travel to reach the slopes of the Himalayas; still more days spent climbing, always climbing, to reach this remote point. And all for nothing.

Soon they would have to turn back, the expedition a failure. Back in London there would be polite sympathy, concealing quiet amusement. Only Mackay would stand by him. Mackay, his oldest and best friend, the only man who had agreed to join his expedition. Yet now it seemed that even Mackay had turned against him. Mackay was laughing at him, screaming insults.

Suddenly Travers jerked fully awake. He really could hear Mackay's voice. It was calling to him. Screaming for help... Travers rubbed his eyes and looked across the circle of light round the camp fire. Mackay's sleeping-bag was empty. There were tracks leading out into the darkness. Travers fumbled for his rifle and struggled from his sleeping-bag. Then he set off towards the sound of Mackay's voice. He scrambled over the edge of the little plateau, and down the rocky slope.

In the darkness ahead of him he could see two struggling figures. One was Mackay. But the other... It was enormous – a giant, shaggy form. Travers tried to call out, but could only produce a sort of croak. Instantly the creature flung Mackay to the ground. It whirled round to attack Travers. He raised his rifle, but before he could fire it was wrenched from his hands. Travers caught a brief glimpse of glowing eyes and savage fangs. Then a blow from a giant, hairy paw smashed him to the ground.

Back at the little camp-site the fire was almost out. The guttering of the flames threw a feeble light on the two empty sleeping-bags. The shadow of a huge shuffling figure fell over the site. Something was tossed contemptuously into the dying fire. It was Mackay's rifle. The barrel was bent almost double, the stock shattered into matchwood. The giant shape moved away and vanished into the night.

Next morning, a little higher on that same Himalayan peak, a wheezing, groaning sound shattered the peace and stillness of the mountain air. An old blue police box appeared from nowhere, transparent at first, but gradually becoming solid. It perched on a snowy ledge, looking completely out of place.

Inside the police box was an ultra-modern control room, with a centre console of complex instruments. There was something very odd about this police box. Somehow it was bigger on the inside than on the outside.

There were three people in the control room. One was a middle-aged, middle-sized man with a gentle, rather comical face, and a shock of untidy black hair. He was wearing an old black coat, and a pair of rather baggy check trousers. Watching him were a brawny youth in highland dress, complete with kilt, and a small, dark girl dressed in the style of Earth's Victorian age. Appropriately enough, since her name was Victoria.

She was the daughter of a Victorian antique dealer, who had lost his life during a terrifying adventure with

3

the Daleks. Alone and friendless, Victoria had been taken under the protection of a mysterious traveller in Space and Time known only as the Doctor.

Much the same thing had happened to Jamie, the Scots lad, whose fate had become caught up with the Doctor's during the Jacobite rebellion. Now both young people, wrenched from their own times, spent their lives travelling through Time and Space with the Doctor in the strangely disguised craft known as the TARDIS. (The Doctor had told Victoria that the initials stood for Time and Relative Dimensions in Space – which left her none the wiser.)

Victoria sometimes wondered if her decision to join the Doctor had been a wise one. He was very kind, in his vague, erratic way, and she was very fond of him. But he did seem to have a knack of wandering into the most appalling danger. Victoria, like most girls of her time, had had a rather sheltered upbringing. Her travels with the Doctor had brought her a number of rather nerve-shattering experiences. But despite her initial timidity, she was discovering unexpected resources of courage inside herself.

Jamie, on the other hand, was completely different. He welcomed each new adventure with tremendous gusto. Jamie was a fighter by nature. English Redcoat soldier or alien monster, it was all the same to Jamie. He grabbed his trusty claymore and charged.

Victoria looked on indulgently as the Doctor peered into the little scanner screen, almost hopping up and down with excitement. As usual, she and Jamie had no idea *where* or *when* they were – or for that matter, *why*. No doubt the Doctor would get round to telling them in his own good time.

'Marvellous,' the Doctor was chortling. 'Absolutely marvellous! And after all this time!' He adjusted the scanner controls and the picture of snowy wastes changed to that of a distinctively-shaped peak.

Jamie looked over the Doctor's shoulder. 'I dinna see what's so marvellous about a lot of snowy mountains.'

The Doctor looked up in amazement. 'But it's the Himalayas, Jamie! The Himalayas!'

'The Hima – what?' Geography wasn't Jamie's strong point. Anywhere outside Scotland was unknown territory to him.

Victoria leaned forward. 'The Himalayas. They're a range of mountains. On the border between India and Tibet, I think.'

The Doctor turned away from the scanner. 'That's right! Tibet, that's where we are. Tibet!' The Doctor beamed at Victoria, then said briskly, 'Well, come on then, no time to waste. Help me find the ghanta.' He rushed across the TARDIS, opened a wall-locker and dragged out an enormous old chest, covered in antique carving. 'Now I'm sure I put it in here somewhere!' The Doctor started ferreting inside the chest, rather like a dog at a rabbit hole, throwing things over his shoulder with gay abandon. Jamie and Victoria looked on in amazement. After a moment, the Doctor's head popped up indignantly. 'Come on, you two. Aren't you going to help me?'

They came over to join him. 'That's all verra well,' said Jamie. 'Can you no' tell us what we're looking for?'

'I've already told you. The ghanta!' The Doctor went on burrowing.

'Yes, but what's a ghanta?' Victoria asked gently.

The Doctor was amazed. 'You mean you don't know? It's a Tibetan holy relic. A bell actually. Quite small. You see it was given to me to look after when…'

The Doctor broke off as he pulled an enormous fur coat from the bottom of the chest. 'Ah,' he exclaimed delightedly, 'now I'll have that. Just the thing for this climate.' The Doctor began to struggle into the coat. It completely swamped him, coming right down to his ankles. 'Tell you what, I'll just go and have a scout around.' Suddenly he couldn't wait to be off.

Jamie looked up from the chest. 'What about this precious ghanta?'

The Doctor looked uneasy. 'Ah. Well, I thought you and Victoria might find it for me.' He looked pleadingly at them, like a small boy begging to be allowed to go out and play.

Victoria smiled. 'All right, Doctor, off you go. We'll find your bell for you. But what do you want it for? Why's it so important?'

The Doctor paused at the door. 'Because when we get down there, it'll guarantee us the welcome of a lifetime.'

'Down *where*?' called Victoria. But the Doctor was

already gone, the door of the TARDIS closing behind him.

Jamie sighed. 'When you've been with the Doctor as long as I have, you'll realise ye canna hope to know what he's talking about most of the time. Let's find his bell, there'll be no peace till we do!'

Jamie went on rummaging in the chest. Victoria wandered over to the scanner and switched it on, hoping to see where the Doctor was off to. Suddenly she jumped back from the screen in terror. 'Jamie, look!'

Jamie came over to the scanner, and peered in amazement at the huge, hairy form on the little screen. 'It's a beastie,' he muttered, 'a huge hairy beastie!'

Victoria felt a sudden stab of fear. 'We must warn the Doctor…'

Jamie held up a restraining hand. 'Just a wee moment. Let's have another look.' He adjusted the scanner controls to give a closer view of the shambling figure. Then he looked up, grinning. 'Ye needna worry about warning the Doctor. Yon great hairy beastie *is* the Doctor!'

And indeed the Doctor did look rather like a huge animal as he plodded up the mountain path in his enormous fur coat. He gazed around him with child-like pleasure.

The surrounding peaks seemed to sparkle in the clear frosty atmosphere. The Doctor took deep, satisfying breaths of the fresh, sharp mountain air, puffing it out again like steam. The path climbed sharply upwards, and soon the Doctor was breathing hard. He reached the point he was making for and leaned thankfully against a boulder. A hidden valley lay far below him. And there nestling in the valley was the Monastery. The Doctor sighed with quiet satisfaction. For once the TARDIS, and his navigation, hadn't let him down. He'd come to exactly the right spot. Clumps of snow had built up on the Doctor's boots, making walking difficult. He began kicking his boots against a boulder to clean them. Suddenly he stopped, his eye caught by something at his feet. It was an enormous footprint, many times the size of his own.

The Doctor began to cast about the area, like a hunting dog. There were other footprints, a line of them, leading to the other side of the boulder. Cautiously, the Doctor followed the tracks. On the other side of the boulder there were more footprints, deeper ones. The snow was churned as though the creature had stood for some time. There were other tracks leading away down the mountainside.

The Doctor stood, pondering. The story in the snow was clear. Some enormous creature had climbed to this spot, and stood there, looking down at the Monastery below. Then it had moved away. Not long ago, either. The tracks leading away from the boulder were still fairly fresh.

The Doctor's scientific curiosity was roused. Could it be – he'd heard the stories, of course, on previous visits to Earth – The Abominable Snowman? Known to the Tibetans as the Yeti. A giant man-like creature that lived somewhere on the remotest peaks, seen only in glimpses by terrified natives. But surely the creature had never been heard of in this part of Tibet? The Doctor was puzzled. For a moment he was strongly tempted to follow the tracks still further.

The Doctor had seen so many amazing creatures on so many planets that he was prepared to believe in anything. Then he checked himself. What would he do with the creature if he found it? Come to that, what would it do with him? There was the Monastery to be visited. And Jamie and Victoria still waiting in the TARDIS. Congratulating himself on his self-control, the Doctor turned and retraced his steps.

Suddenly he stopped. Had there been a flash of movement, higher up the mountain? There, behind the clump of boulders? The Doctor peered, but could see nothing. He continued on his way, back to the TARDIS.

Behind those same boulders there was a stir of movement. An enormous hairy hand appeared on the top of a sheltering boulder. A giant, shaggy form pulled itself upright. It stood looking down at the tiny figure of the Doctor, plodding on his way far below.

Jamie rose from the empty trunk in disgust. 'He must have put this ghanta thing somewhere else. It's no' in here!'

Victoria looked round at the amazing collection of objects spread over the TARDIS floor: clothes, weapons, curios and carvings from a hundred different planets. There was something of the magpie in the Doctor, she thought despairingly. 'Are you sure the trunk's empty? Really empty?'

'Och, see for yourself!'

Victoria groped in the inner recesses of the enormous trunk, practically disappearing inside. 'I'm afraid you're – wait a minute!' Her fingers touched a scrap of cloth wedged in a corner. Stretching, she pulled a tiny bundle from the trunk. 'Look, there's a label on it. "Ghanta of Det-sen Monastery."' Victoria unwrapped the bundle. Triumphantly, she held up an ornately carved bronze bell.

'Wouldn't you know it'd be the verra last thing?' groaned Jamie disgustedly. The TARDIS door opened and the Doctor came in. He saw the little bell in Victoria's hand.

'Found it, have you? Splendid. Knew it wasn't far away.' Gently he took it from Victoria and slipped it in his pocket.

'It took a wee bit of searching, ye ken,' said Jamie dryly.

The Doctor frowned abstractedly. 'Yes, I'm sure it did...'

Jamie looked at him. 'You've seen something, haven't you? Out there?'

The Doctor glanced quickly at Victoria. 'Oh, nothing really, Jamie. Probably nothing.' He came to a decision. 'I've just got to pay a quick visit to the Monastery, and then we'll be on our way. Stay here in the TARDIS, will you, Jamie?'

'Would it no' be better if I came too?'

The Doctor shook his head. Victoria looked from one to the other. 'Look, what's happening? Is there something dangerous out there?'

The Doctor smiled. 'Just a lot of snow! I'll be as quick as I can.' The Doctor left the TARDIS, closing the door behind him.

Victoria turned to Jamie. 'There is something the matter, isn't there?'

Jamie nodded reluctantly. 'Something's worrying him, right enough. But don't go asking me what, for I dinna ken!'

Victoria looked at the litter of objects on the floor. 'Come on, Jamie. Let's put this lot away.'

The Doctor was slowly picking his way along the uneven track that led down towards the Monastery. Every now and again he would stop, looking around him uneasily. He kept getting the feeling that something malevolent and hostile was watching his every movement. Sometimes he thought he saw a flicker of movement on the slopes above him. But always it vanished before he could pin it down. Warily the Doctor plodded on his way.

He followed the path round the curve of the mountain, and on to a little plateau. It formed a kind of natural camp-site, and the Doctor saw that someone had indeed made camp there. A few charred sticks marked the remains of a fire. Close by were two empty sleeping-bags. Something glinted in the cold ashes of the fire. The Doctor fished it out. It was the barrel of a rifle, bent almost double. The charred, splintered stock was burnt almost completely away. The Doctor wondered what kind of strength could bend the steel of a rifle barrel like plasticine.

Footprints, human footprints, led over the edge of the plateau. Peering over the edge, the Doctor saw a huddled shape a little further down. He scrambled towards it.

The body lay face down in the snow. Gently the Doctor turned it over. To his surprise he saw that the man was a European. As he shifted the body, the head lolled over at a strange angle. The man was dead, his neck broken by a single savage blow.

2

The Creature in the Cave

The Doctor straightened up, and stood looking down at the body. For a moment he considered going straight back to the TARDIS. All around him he sensed the presence of some alien evil. Then he remembered the ghanta.

Slipping his hand in his pocket, the Doctor took out the little Tibetan bell. He gazed at it for a moment, and sighed. A promise was a promise. But as soon as he had returned the ghanta to the Monastery, he would go back to the TARDIS and whisk Jamie and Victoria off to a safer place and time. Not far from the dead man, a rucksack lay in the snow. It held maps, warm clothes, brandy, concentrated foods – the provisions of an experienced explorer. Perhaps he would find the owner at the Monastery – if he had survived the attack on the camp.

After a long and weary journey, the Doctor finally reached the lower slopes of the mountain. The path sloped sharply, leading him at last to the Det-sen Monastery. With a sigh of relief, he looked up at the huge old building he remembered so well. Protected by its high stone walls, the Monastery huddled as if for shelter in the valley between two mountains. It had been many years since his last visit, yet nothing had changed. Or had it? In former days, the massive bronze doors had always stood open, welcoming the entry of pilgrims and travellers. The monks of Det-sen were peaceful, hospitable men, always willing to provide shelter. But now the gates were closed. An oppressive silence seemed to hang over the Monastery.

The Doctor took a deep breath. 'Hello! Hello! Anyone about?' His voice echoed round the high forbidding walls. He hammered on the doors, but his fists made almost no sound. The Doctor put his shoulder to the heavy, bronze doors and shoved – more as a kind of gesture than with any hope of success. To his surprise, he felt them shift a little. Using all his strength, he managed to push one of the doors ajar, creating just enough of a gap to slip through. Once through the doors, the Doctor gazed round him. The long rectangular courtyard was unchanged. The stone flagstones were worn smooth by the sandalled feet of generations of monks. Doorways and cloisters led off into different parts of the rambling old Monastery. But still this mysterious silence and emptiness. The Det-sen Monastery had always buzzed like a beehive – the chatter of pilgrims, the cries of pedlars in the courtyard, the low humming of the temple bells, the endless drone of the monks at their prayers. It had been a lively, bustling place. Now it was as quiet as a tomb. The Doctor shivered. He walked to the middle of the courtyard, his footsteps echoing hollowly. 'Hello!

Where *is* everyone?'

Suddenly there came a shattering clang. The Doctor whirled round. The bronze doors had been pushed to, and barred. A little group of men stood watching him. They wore the simple robes of the Det-sen monks, but they carried bows and swords. They ran forward and surrounded the Doctor, weapons raised.

Their leader, a tall man with a dark, hawk-like face, towered over him.

'Who are you? Why do you come here?'

Quite unintimidated, the Doctor smiled up at him. 'First may I ask *who* you are? By what right do you question me?'

'I am Khrisong, leader of the warrior monks.' The tall man indicated a younger monk who stood at his side. 'This is Thomni – my guard captain. Now – you will answer. Who are you?'

Gently the Doctor said, 'You can call me the Doctor.' He looked at the group. 'Warrior monks – that's a contradiction in terms, isn't it? I thought the monks of Det-sen were men of peace.'

There was grim irony in Khrisong's reply. 'Most of them still are. But these are dangerous times. If the men of peace are to survive, they need men of war to protect them.' His tone hardened. 'Now – you would do well to answer quickly. Who are you? What is your business at the Monastery of Det-sen?'

Before the Doctor could answer a man ran out of the cloisters and up to the little group. He flung himself on

15

the Doctor, wrenching the rucksack from his shoulders.

'You murderous devil. We've got you now!'

The Doctor looked curiously at his attacker. He was a European, dressed in a ragged, travel-stained anorak. His eyes were red-rimmed with exhaustion, and a stubble of beard covered his chin. His manner was hysterical, like a man in the grip of some over-mastering obsession. He glared angrily at the Doctor.

Khrisong turned to the newcomer. 'Travers! Do you know this man?'

'No – but this rucksack's mine all right. He must have stolen it when he attacked my camp.' Travers hugged the rucksack protectively.

'You told us that a beast attacked you,' said Khrisong sharply.

'Well, that's what I thought. I just saw a shape in the darkness – felt the fur. But look at his coat! That's what I felt. It *must* have been him. How else did he get my rucksack?'

The little group of armed men gathered menacingly round the Doctor. 'Why did you attack this man?' snapped Khrisong.

The Doctor kept his voice low and calm. 'I attacked no one. I found this rucksack by a wrecked camp. There was a dead man—'

'Yes – and you killed him!' shrieked Travers. Dropping the rucksack, he hurled himself at the Doctor. Thomni and another of the warrior monks held him back.

Khrisong said, 'We have heard enough. Seize him!'

Before the Doctor could move, two brawny young monks had grabbed his arms.

'Look,' said the Doctor mildly, 'this is ridiculous. I've killed no one. I brought the rucksack here to return it to its owner. I came on a most important...'

'Silence,' interrupted Khrisong. 'You have been accused of a crime. There have been many other such crimes of late. All strangers are suspect. If you are guilty, be sure you will be punished. Take him away!'

Lifting him almost off his feet, the two warrior monks carried the protesting Doctor away. At a nod from Khrisong, Thomni released Travers. He seized Khrisong's arm, looking up at the tall monk with a kind of crazy intentness. 'He's a dangerous man, Khrisong. Watch him carefully!'

Thomni, the young guard captain, said thoughtfully, 'We do not *know* that this man is the killer...'

'Of course we do,' Travers interrupted. 'I've just told you so.'

Thomni ignored him. 'After all,' he went on, 'we still do not know *why* he came here.'

'That, too, we shall discover – in good time,' said Khrisong impassively.

The two warrior monks half-carried, half-dragged the Doctor along the endless stone corridors of the Monastery, ignoring his spirited protests. 'Do put me down, you chaps. I can walk, you know. Anyway, I've got something important to tell you...'

The monks came to a halt before a massive wooden

door, studded with iron. They opened it, thrust the Doctor inside, slammed the door and bolted it. Then they turned and marched away.

The Doctor looked around him. He was in a bare stone cell, with a little window high up in the wall. There was a wooden stool, and a wooden bed with a straw mattress along one wall. The Doctor sank down on the bed and sighed. He remembered his own words, back in the TARDIS. 'The welcome of a lifetime!' said the Doctor ruefully.

Jamie and Victoria sat looking at each other blankly. The contents of the massive chest had been tidied away long ago. Now they were just sitting waiting – and waiting. Jamie gave a massive yawn.

'I'm getting very bored,' Victoria said. 'Couldn't we take a look outside?'

Jamie shook his head. 'The Doctor said to wait here.'

'I'll go by myself.' Victoria stood up decisively.

Jamie sighed. It was in the nature of females to be contrary. 'Och, all right. Just a wee look round. We'd better wrap up warm.'

Victoria gave him a happy smile, and rushed to the TARDIS' clothing locker, which held garments in every imaginable size to suit every possible climate. Soon the two of them were kitted out like polar explorers in warm, fur-lined anoraks, with fur gloves and fur-lined boots.

Victoria rushed to the door. 'Come on, Jamie!'

'Just a wee moment.' Jamie went back to the big chest,

and rummaged inside. He fished out a huge curved sword – a kind of Turkish scimitar.

'What on earth do you want that for?'

'Aye, well, ye never know what ye'll run in to.' Grasping the sword firmly, Jamie ushered Victoria outside. If there was something dangerous out there, he was ready for it.

Standing on the little ledge, Victoria looked entranced at the panorama of mountain scenery spread out before them. 'Look how clear everything is, Jamie. Even the furthest peaks seem close enough to touch. Aren't the Himalayas beautiful?'

'Aye, well, they're no' so bad.' As far as Jamie was concerned there were bigger and better mountains at home in Scotland.

'Let's climb a little higher, Jamie. Maybe we'll see the Doctor coming back.'

They scrambled up the mountain track, which became steeper and narrower. Suddenly Victoria stopped. 'Jamie, look!' She pointed downwards. Just to one side of the path was an area of churned-up snow. Leading away from it was a set of enormous footprints. They stooped to examine them.

Jamie whistled. 'Will you look at the size of that? Something's been prowling round here, right enough. A bear, mebbe.'

Suddenly Victoria gave a little gasp of excitement. 'Jamie! Perhaps it's the Yeti – the Abominable Snowman!'

'The abominable what?'

'There have been stories and legends about them in the Himalayas for ages. Huge furry creatures. Something between a bear, an ape and a man. Let's track it, Jamie!'

'We will not! Look at those footprints. Ye can see how big the beastie must be.'

Victoria jumped up and down in excitement. 'You don't understand, Jamie. People have been trying to find the Abominable Snowman for ages. Scientific expeditions and everything. No one's succeeded. It'd be marvellous if we found it.'

'That's all verra well. Suppose it finds us first?'

'There's nothing to worry about, Jamie. All the reports say it's a timid creature. It'll run as soon as it sees us.' Jamie still looked dubious. Cunningly, Victoria continued, 'Of course, if you're *afraid*...'

Jamie was outraged. 'Me? Afraid? I'll have you know, my girl, we Highlanders fear nothing. Come on!' Brandishing his sword, Jamie set off. Victoria smiled to herself, and followed him.

The trail of huge footprints led them higher and higher up the mountain slope. They scrambled over boulders and across icy patches. The creature they were following was obviously strong and agile, able to move over the roughest ground. Eventually, the tracks led them straight into the side of the mountain. They found themselves at the entrance to a small cave. 'Well, there you are then,' said Jamie. 'That's where the beastie lives.'

Victoria peered curiously into the darkness of the cave mouth. Just to the right of it stood a huge boulder, just a little larger than the cave mouth itself. 'It looks almost like a door,' said Victoria. 'Couldn't we just have a quick look inside the cave?'

'And mebbe wake the beastie up? We'll do no such thing. Come on, my girl, it's back to the TARDIS for us.' Obediently Victoria started back down the mountainside. On second thoughts, she was rather pleased not to be going inside that dark cave. There was something rather spooky about it. Suddenly she realised that Jamie wasn't following her. He had moved closer to the cave entrance, and was looking inside.

'Hey, Victoria, look at this. Just inside the cave. Wooden beams!'

Victoria came to join him. Intrigued, Jamie went up to the cave entrance. 'Aye, it's beams, right enough. Kind of supports. Mebbe this thing we're following is no' a beastie after all.' And before Victoria could stop him, Jamie plunged into the darkness of the cave.

'Come back, Jamie,' she called. 'You said we should go back to the TARDIS.'

Jamie's voice came from within the cave, booming hollowly. 'That was when I thought we were tracking a wild animal. I'm no' afraid of a *man*.'

Victoria decided that she was more frightened of being left outside than of going in. She followed Jamie into the cave. Actually it turned out to be more of a tunnel leading into the heart of the mountain, just inside the entrance the walls were supported by what looked like pit-props. They could see other props further down the tunnel. Jamie examined the nearest beam curiously. 'Now what kind of a beastie builds a thing like this?'

There came a grinding noise from the cave entrance. A huge shadow fell across the light, blocking it out completely. Suddenly they were in darkness. Victoria clutched Jamie's arm in fear. 'What is it? What's happened?'

It took Jamie a moment to work things out. Then he realised. 'You remember yon big rock by the entrance… the one you said looked like a door?' Victoria nodded. 'Well,' said Jamie grimly, 'someone's just shut that door!'

Outside the cave, two huge hairy paws finished jamming the boulder into place. Then a massive shaggy form turned and lumbered away down the mountainside.

By dragging the wooden bed under the window, putting the wooden stool on the bed, and climbing on top of the stool, the Doctor was just able to peer out of the high barred window of his cell. He looked down on the courtyard far below. He grasped the bars and shook them but they were set firmly in the stone-framed window.

There was a rattle from behind the Doctor, and a barred grille in his cell door slid open. He turned and saw the face of Travers peering through at him.

'It's a forty-foot drop down there, you know,' said Travers. 'There's no way out.'

The Doctor clambered down from his perch. 'I didn't really think there would be.' He smiled placidly at Travers, who glared back at him, and asked fiercely, 'How did you track me down?'

'My dear chap, I don't even know who you are.'

There was a sharp note of hysteria in Travers' reply. 'Don't you play the innocent with me. You all laughed at me, didn't you? "Travers, the mad anthropologist!" And now that I'm close to success, you want to steal my glory. Just as I've found them at last.'

'Found what?'

'You know what I'm talking about. They're here, on this mountain. The Yeti – the Abominable Snowmen.'

The Doctor nodded. 'Yes, I rather thought they might be. But don't you see, my dear fellow, that makes nonsense of your accusing me. Obviously, a Yeti attacked your camp.'

'Nonsense! The Yeti are timid, harmless creatures. Everyone knows that.'

The Doctor tried another tack. 'Whoever – whatever – attacked your camp and killed your poor friend must have had enormous strength. Isn't that so?'

Reluctantly, Travers nodded. The Doctor rose to his modest height and spread out his hands. 'Well, could I have done it? Could I? Just look at me!' The Doctor could almost see the self-evident truth of this statement fighting to get through to Travers' brain. All at once, a look of childish cunning came over Travers' face. 'Not going to discuss it any longer. I've got work to do. And as for you, while you're safely locked up here, you won't be able to steal my credit.' Abruptly Travers' face disappeared and the grille slammed shut. The Doctor sighed, stretched out on the hard, lumpy mattress, and prepared for a little doze.

At that very moment, the Doctor was the subject of fierce discussion. In the nearby Great Hall, Khrisong and Thomni were confronting a group of older men in saffron-coloured robes. These were lamas, the priests of Det-sen Monastery, whose lives were spent in peaceful meditation and prayer. Despite their gentle and unworldly manner they had a sort of spiritual strength, a kind of gentle obstinacy, that never failed to infuriate Khrisong. He leaned forward urgently in an attempt to carry his point.

'We have the word of the Englishman, Travers. Why should he lie?'

Sapan, oldest and wisest of the lamas said gently, 'The man Travers has had a most terrible experience. His mind has been affected. The man is consumed with fear and ambition. He has strayed far from the way of truth!'

Khrisong's voice was fierce. 'The death of Travers' companion is the latest of many deaths. You know how many of our brethren have been killed. We live in terror. The Abbot has sent away most of the brethren to other monasteries for their own safety. The pilgrims, the travellers, the merchants come no more to Det-sen. Only a handful of us remain. My warriors, who fear nothing – and you…' Khrisong broke off in confusion.

Rinchen, another old monk, smiled gently. 'We who

are so old and feeble and useless that death holds no terrors.'

Khrisong said gruffly, 'I mean no disrespect, holy one. You know that all I have said is true.'

'Indeed it is, my son. But we agreed, did we not, that the Yeti were the cause of all our troubles?'

'True, Rinchen. And we wondered why. They were so rarely seen, so timid. Suddenly they became savage. Now here is this stranger, and Travers accuses him. I ask you again, let me put this man to the proof.'

Sapan shook his head. 'You ask us to condemn a man to almost certain death.'

'I am chief warrior. It is my duty to protect you.'

'Not by taking a man's life,' said Sapan firmly. 'You cannot use a human as live bait.'

Khrisong leaped to his feet. 'If it is necessary – yes, I demand that you…'

Sapan spoke quietly as always, but there was an authority in his voice that made Khrisong fall silent. 'No, Khrisong. The price is too high.' There was a murmur of assent from the other lamas, which was interrupted by the boom of a temple gong.

'Come, my brothers,' said Sapan placidly. 'It is time for prayer.' He turned to Khrisong. 'After our meditations, I shall consult with the Abbot.' The little group of lamas filed from the room. Once they were gone, Khrisong exploded with rage.

'This is madness. Must more of our brothers die before we act?'

Thomni looked at him in astonishment. 'But the holy ones have decided. There is no other way.'

'There is for me,' said Khrisong. 'Let them meditate. Let them consult. I, Khrisong will act. Bring me the prisoner!'

Panting with exhaustion, Jamie abandoned his attempt to shift the boulder that blocked their exit. 'Och, it's no use. I canna shift it at all.' Victoria shivered beside him in the darkness, wishing desperately that they'd never left the TARDIS.

'Jamie, what are we going to do now?'

Jamie considered. What was it that the Doctor was always on about? The exercise of logical thought. 'Well, since we canna go back, and we dinna want to stay here – we'll just have to go forward, or rather I will. There's mebbe another exit!'

'But there might be more of those things in there.'

'Aye, there might. That's why I want you to wait here. Just yell if you need me.'

'Don't worry,' said Victoria. 'I'll yell all right.'

Jamie gave her an encouraging pat on the shoulder. Gripping his sword tightly, he set off down the dark tunnel.

For quite a while he had to feel his way along the walls. Then, to his astonishment, he saw a gleam of light ahead of him. Not daylight, though. More a kind of eerie glow. Summoning up all his courage, he moved towards it. As the glow grew brighter he saw that it came from the entrance to some kind of chamber leading off the tunnel. Jamie moved to the entrance, and then stepped inside, looking round in wonder.

He was in a completely circular cave with smooth stone walls. In the centre of the cave stood the source of the light – a little pile of silver spheres, arranged as a pyramid. Each of the spheres was glowing gently, and their combined radiance lit up the cave. Wonderingly, Jamie approached the spheres. He was just reaching out to touch one when a sudden scream echoed down the tunnel.

'Jamie! Jamie, come back!' He turned and ran down the tunnel towards the sound of Victoria's voice.

As he dashed up to her he saw that a rim of light was appearing around the edge of the boulder. He could hear the noise of rock grinding on rock. 'It's coming back,' whispered Victoria fearfully. 'It's taking away the boulder.'

'Aye, that it is,' said Jamie. 'You flatten yourself against the wall. It'll likely go past without seeing you.'

'But what about you?'

Jamie hefted his sword. 'I'll give yon beastie a welcome it doesna expect.'

Jamie backed away as the boulder was swung completely clear. Light flooded into the tunnel, silhouetting the enormous shaggy figure in the cave mouth. With a blood-curdling roar, claws outstretched, it bore down on Jamie. Gripping his sword in both hands, the Highlander brought it round in a savage

slashing cut that should have struck the beast's head from its shoulders. But to Jamie's amazement the sword simply bounced off, as though the creature was made of steel. The Yeti lunged forward, wrenched the sword from Jamie's grasp, and snapped it in two like a matchstick. Remorselessly the Yeti lumbered forward, clawed hands outstretched to grasp him…

3

Live Bait to Catch a Monster

Jamie backed away before the advancing Yeti. 'Stay back, Victoria!' he yelled. 'I canna stop it!' Terrified of being separated from Jamie, Victoria edged along the wall of the tunnel. She was actually following behind the Yeti, which didn't seem to have noticed her. Jamie retreated along the tunnel as far as the inner cave. Trying to run backwards, he crashed full into one of the pit-props supporting the tunnel. A trickle of rubble fell from the tunnel roof. The Yeti suddenly stopped, as if alarmed by the falling rock.

Jamie flung his arms round the base of the loose beam and pulled with all his might. It shifted! There was a steady rumble as more rubble trickled down. Victoria shrieked, 'No, Jamie, don't! We'll be buried alive.' But Jamie ignored her. With a final mighty heave he wrenched the supporting beam free. A cascade of rock began pouring down from the roof. 'Back, Victoria, back!' yelled Jamie.

With Victoria on one side, and Jamie on the other, the great pile of falling rock landed neatly on the Yeti between them, burying the creature completely, except for one paw, which stuck out from under the pile.

Dust filled the tunnel as the rock stopped falling at last. Coughing and spluttering, Jamie called, 'Victoria! Where are you? Are you all right?' To his vast relief he heard the sound of more coughing. Dimly he saw Victoria's dust-covered form clambering over the rocks towards him. He grabbed her arm and led her into the little inner chamber. Victoria dusted herself down in an attempt to recover her composure.

'That horrible creature,' she gasped. 'What was it?'

'I dinna ken, lassie. But it was verra strong. Did you see what it did to my sword?' said Jamie indignantly.

Looking round the cave Victoria saw the pyramid of spheres. 'What *are* those things?'

Jamie picked one up, and hefted it in his hand. 'Feels like some kind of metal…'

Victoria suddenly shivered. 'Jamie, let's get out of here.'

Jamie nodded. 'We're lucky that rock-fall didna block the whole tunnel!'

Slipping the sphere into his pocket, Jamie grabbed Victoria's hand and pulled her out of the cave, back towards the pile of rock. For a moment she hung back, afraid to go too near the buried Yeti.

'Dinna be afraid,' said Jamie reassuringly. 'The thing's dead right enough! Nothing could survive a ton of rock on its head.'

Victoria clambered over the pile of rocks, keeping as far away as she could from the projecting hand. Suddenly she screamed and clutched at Jamie. 'Look!'

The Yeti's hand was clenching and unclenching slowly, as if making an attempt to grab her. Before their horrified gaze, the hand, and part of the arm, began to wriggle out of the pile of rocks. The creature was alive, and struggling to free itself.

'Come on!' said Jamie grimly. He almost dragged Victoria over the rocks, down the tunnel and out into the open air.

Victoria looked round in amazement. 'It's starting to get dark. We were in there for ages.'

For a moment the two of them stood gasping, drawing the sharp, fresh air into their lungs. From inside the cave came a rumble of rock, and then the savage roar of the Yeti. 'Come on,' said Jamie. 'It'll be after us any minute.'

They began running down the mountain slope, towards the TARDIS.

Thomni the guard captain was a worried young man as he went along the corridor towards the Doctor's cell. He could sympathise with Khrisong's impatience. The lamas didn't realise that not every problem could be solved by prayer and meditation. But even so, to disobey the will of the holy ones in the way that Khrisong was planning...

Thomni unbolted the door of the cell, and threw it open. The stranger was sleeping peacefully on the bed. Thomni looked down at him. The face was gentle and relaxed with something of the serenity of the holy ones themselves about it. Thomni jumped, as the man on the bed spoke without opening his eyes. 'Have you come to release me?'

Thomni felt strangely at a disadvantage. 'Er, no... sir.'

The Doctor sat up on the bed and beamed at him. 'It's Thomni, isn't it? Captain of the Guard? By the way, I'm usually called "The Doctor".'

Somehow the name was familiar to Thomni. 'You must come with me, Doctor,' he said.

'Let's have a little chat first, shall we?'

'Khrisong is waiting...'

'What's come over this place?' asked the Doctor plaintively. 'No one wants to listen to me. You seem a reasonable sort of lad. What's going on, eh? Why is everything so military? You'd think there was a war on.'

'So there is – and we are besieged. The Yeti have turned on us. At least, that is what we thought until...' Thomni stopped, confused.

'Until I turned up. And friend Khrisong decided, on very slender evidence, that it's all my fault. You know, the last time I visited Det-sen, there was trouble. Something about a threatened attack by Chinese bandits.'

Thomni stared at him in amazement. 'You must be mistaken. That attack was many hundreds of years ago... It was then that the holy ghanta was lost.'

The Doctor smiled. 'Indeed? What happened to it?'

'It is hard to be sure. Some say that it was stolen by the bandits when they attacked. But there is a legend that it was given to a mysterious stranger for safe-keeping. One

34

known only as—'

'As the Doctor?' interrupted the man on the bed.

Thomni nodded, surprised. 'I see you have studied our history. The legend tells us that the stranger swore to return it. Yet he warned that this might not happen for many hundreds of years…' Thomni stopped, puzzled. 'You said *you* were called the Doctor!'

The cell burst open and Khrisong entered, armed monks at his back. 'Why this delay? Seize him and take him to the gate!'

The monks grabbed the Doctor and pulled him to his feet. As he was bustled out of the cell, he stumbled against Thomni. To his astonishment, Thomni heard the Doctor whisper, 'Under straw, in the mattress – tell Abbot…' Before he could say more, the Doctor was dragged away, down the corridor.

Thomni stood puzzled. He went to the bed and examined the straw mattress. Just where the Doctor had been sitting, a little hole had been picked. Thomni felt inside. His fingers touched a little cloth-wrapped bundle. He pulled it out, and unwrapped it. There in his hand was the holy ghanta of Det-sen. The ghanta which had been lost for over three hundred years.

Hand in hand, Jamie and Victoria pelted down the mountainside. Every now and again, Victoria managed a quick glance over her shoulder, but the creature from the cave didn't seem to be following them. All the same, she sighed with relief when at last they came in sight of the

TARDIS. Soon they would be safe.

But as they ran towards the TARDIS, a huge shaggy shape could be seen in the gloom. Jamie and Victoria skidded to a halt. 'It's here before us,' gasped Victoria. 'But how *can* it be – we'd have seen it.'

'Then it canna be the same beastie,' said Jamie. 'There's more than one of them!'

Jamie studied the creature cautiously, fascinated by his first clear look at a Yeti. It was massive, about seven or eight feet tall, Jamie guessed, and covered in shaggy, brown fur. The powerful body was immensely broad, so that the thing seemed somehow squat and lumpy, in spite of its great height.

The huge hairy hands, and the black snout, were gorilla-like. The little red eyes, and the yellow fangs were like those of a bear. He remembered Victoria's description – something between a bear, an ape and a man. All in all, thought Jamie, it was the biggest, nastiest, hairiest beastie he had ever seen.

Victoria tugged urgently at his arm. 'Jamie, what are we going to do?' Jamie looked again at the Yeti. It was making no attempt to attack them, though they were now quite close. It stood like a kind of weird sentry, quite motionless, waiting.

Jamie rubbed his chin. 'Well, we canna get back into the TARDIS, yon beastie's blocking the way. We'll just have to go on – down to this Monastery place. Maybe we can find the Doctor and warn him what's going on.'

Now too exhausted to run, Jamie and Victoria stumbled down the mountainside towards the Monastery.

In the Monastery courtyard, dusk was falling. The Doctor, guarded by armed warrior monks, stood shivering inside his fur coat. He was the subject of a heated argument between the old lama, Sapan, and a very angry Khrisong.

'Do not interfere, holy one,' said the warrior monk furiously.

Sapan's voice was gentle as always. 'Did we not agree, Khrisong, that we would consult the Abbot Songtsen, before taking further action in this matter?'

'No, holy one, we did not agree!' Khrisong said bitterly. 'You decided, as always. But I tell you, I cannot always wait to consult the Abbot before I act.'

'Be reasonable, Khrisong…'

The Doctor stopped listening as the argument raged on. He thought wryly that no one wanted to know what *he* thought, even though his fate was under discussion. Not that he was worried. Once that boy got the sacred ghanta to the Abbot, Songtsen would put a stop to whatever nonsense Khrisong was planning. Something about a test, as far as the Doctor could make out.

A curiously furtive movement caught the corner of the Doctor's eye. He turned and saw Travers about to slip out of the main door. He was fully kitted-out for travel, a loaded rucksack on his back.

'Travers!' the Doctor called. 'Don't you think all this has gone far enough?' He indicated the arguing monks, the armed guards at his elbow. 'For Heaven's sake, tell them you were mistaken.'

Travers shook his head. 'Sorry, nothing I can do.'

'What do you expect to gain by all this?'

'Time,' said Travers fiercely. 'Time to find the Yeti, even though I'm on my own. You won't get another chance to get in my way. *Your* little expedition stops right here.'

The Doctor was indignant. 'I am not an expedition, and I'm not interested in your precious Yeti. But you've put me in a very nasty position. These chaps are liable to do something silly.'

Travers laughed. 'Don't worry, the monks won't harm you. They're men of peace.' Settling his rucksack on his shoulders, Travers turned away, and slipped through the main door, disappearing into the evening shadows.

The Doctor turned back to the arguing monks, just in time to hear Khrisong say, 'I tell you the stranger is a killer. We have Travers' word for that. I believe this man may have found some way to control the Yeti, and make them savage. I shall tie him to the main doors. If the Yeti come to rescue him, my warriors will be waiting...'

'You cannot use a human being as live bait,' Sapan protested.

Overriding the old lama, Khrisong turned to the Doctor's guards. 'Take him outside, and tie him to the door.'

Cupping the ghanta in reverent hands, Thomni crept

timidly into the ante-chamber of the Abbot Songtsen. He looked around him in fear and wonder. He had never dared enter this part of the Monastery before. The room was dimly lit by the prayer lamps. There were no windows. All around were ornate carvings, statues and hangings. Many of the treasures of Det-sen Monastery were here, sacred objects of immense value, treasured and worshipped through the ages. But none were so valuable, or so holy, as the little bronze bell, the ghanta, that Thomni held.

Thomni froze like a statue as the door of the Inner Sanctum creaked open, apparently by itself. This was the most sacred place of all, the very heart of the Monastery. The Abbot Songtsen emerged. Terrified, Thomni prostrated himself. The Abbot backed away from the Sanctum doors, which closed behind him. He turned and crossed the Anteroom, his wise, wrinkled old face still and trance-like. He seemed not even to notice Thomni, and would have walked right past him. Thomni managed to produce a terrified whisper, 'Master Abbot!' Songtsen stopped, consciousness slowly returning to his face. 'Master Abbot!' Thomni whispered again.

A look of horror came over the old man's face as he saw the boy crouching at his feet. 'Thomni – you know well that only I may enter this sacred place.'

Silently, Thomni held out his hands, the ghanta cupped in their palms. The Abbot leaned forward and peered at the little bell. 'What is this? Where did you get it?'

Thomni's voice was low and reverent. 'Master Abbot, is this not the sacred ghanta which was lost?'

Suddenly another voice spoke. It came from nowhere, and yet from everywhere in the room. It was old and wise, yet strong and vigorous too. The voice said, 'It is indeed the holy ghanta, my son. Lost to us for three hundred years. How came you by it?'

Terrified, Thomni looked round for the source of the voice. But, apart from himself and the Abbot, the Anteroom was empty. Yet the power of the speaker's personality filled the entire room. Too frightened to speak, Thomni looked to the Abbot, who said gently, 'It is the Master, Padmasambvha. Do not be afraid.'

The voice spoke again. 'Bring the ghanta to me – both of you.' The Abbot bowed his head in assent, and indicated that Thomni should follow him. Thomni scrambled to his feet, and followed the Abbot through the door to the Inner Sanctum. The doors opened silently as they approached.

The handles of the great doors of Det-sen Monastery were in the form of huge, bronze rings. To one of these rings, the Doctor was being firmly lashed with leather thongs. Khrisong gave a final check to the knots, and nodded in satisfaction. He turned to the little group of warriors around him. 'Place yourself at the windows, on the walls, and in cover behind the doors. Be ready with your bows.' As the warrior monks went off to take their places Khrisong looked grimly at the Doctor. 'If your servants attempt to rescue you, we shall slay them!'

The Doctor sighed wearily. 'This is all very pointless, you know. I assure you, no one's going to rescue me – least of all an Abominable Snowman.' Khrisong turned to go back inside the Monastery. 'And there's something else,' yelled the Doctor. 'Does it occur to you that whatever has been killing your monks might also kill me?'

Khrisong said ironically, 'If the Yeti attack *you*, that will be proof of your innocence. Then, of course, we shall rescue you – if we can.' He turned and went back inside the Monastery.

The Doctor sighed wearily. 'This is all very point—' and then gave up. It was almost dark now, and gloomy shadows covered the mountain path and the area before the Monastery doors. Everything looked odd and sinister in the half-light. The Doctor wondered what was happening to Thomni. Perhaps he hadn't even found the ghanta. And what about Jamie and Victoria? They must be getting pretty bored by now…

Jamie and Victoria were far too frightened to be bored. It was no easy task, picking their way down to the Monastery in the fast-gathering gloom. Several times they had wandered off the snow-covered path, finding their way back only with difficulty. As the gloom thickened and the shadows grew darker and longer, every rock and boulder seemed a Yeti waiting to pounce.

Victoria clasped Jamie's hand tighter and wailed, 'Oh, Jamie, I'm sure we're lost again.'

Jamie did his best to sound confident. 'I tell you we canna be lost. The path leads down the mountain, and the Monastery's at the bottom. All we've got to do is keep going.'

But Victoria wasn't listening. She stopped and whispered, 'There's something moving. Ahead of us, down there.'

Jamie sighed. 'Ever since we set off, you've been seeing things…'

'I'm not imagining it this time. Listen!'

Jamie peered through the gloom, straining his ears. Sure enough, there was something… a sound of shuffling feet, and heavy breathing. Jamie looked round for a weapon. He grabbed a football-sized rock from the side of the path, and stood poised and ready. A shadowy figure loomed up out of the darkness, huge and threatening. Victoria gave a little scream and Jamie was just about to let fly, when the figure spoke. 'Hey, you two! What are you doing here?'

Jamie dropped the rock with a sigh of relief. The figure came nearer and was revealed as a man wearing a rucksack. But Jamie was still cautious. 'I might ask you the same,' he said stoutly.

'My name's Travers. I'm a sort of explorer.'

'We're on our way to the Monastery,' said Victoria.

'Are you now? You wouldn't be anything to do with a feller calls himself the Doctor, would you?'

'Aye, that we would,' said Jamie. 'Have you seen him? Is he all right?'

The man laughed. 'Oh yes, I met him at the Monastery. He's perfectly all right.'

'Come on, Jamie, we'd better go and find him,' said Victoria.

'Yes, why don't you do that,' said the man. 'I expect the monks will give you quite a welcome.' He nodded and set off up the path.

Jamie hesitated. He hadn't taken to the man at all. His eyes were bright and feverish, and there was something odd about his manner. All the same, it was only fair to warn him.

Jamie called after the retreating figure. 'I'd watch your step, Mister, if I were you. There's some kind of great hairy beasties prowling about. They live in a cave higher up the mountains.'

The man turned and ran back towards them. 'You've seen the Yeti? You've actually found their lair?' He grabbed Jamie's arm and tried to pull him off by force. 'You've got to take me there. Now, right away.'

Jamie pulled his arm away firmly. 'I will not. I've seen enough of those things to last a lifetime.'

'But I've got to find them. I've got to.' Travers was almost babbling with excitement.

Jamie was unmoved. 'Ye canna go up there now, man. It's nearly dark. I couldna find the place myself.'

'Will you take me there tomorrow?'

'Aye, mebbe. But on one condition.'

Travers glared at him suspiciously. 'What's that, then?'

'You say you've come from the Monastery?'

Travers nodded.

'Then you can just guide us back there – now. That's if you want my help tomorrow.'

Travers hesitated, obviously still wanting to get after the Yeti right away. But it *was* nearly dark. And if this boy had found their lair...

'All right, then. Come on.' Travers turned and set off back down the path.

Jamie took Victoria's arm and gave her a reassuring grin. They both hurried off after their guide. Travers waited for Jamie to catch up and said, 'Tell me exactly where you found this cave...'

The Inner Sanctum was even darker and more mysterious than the Anteroom. In its centre was a raised dais, upon which was set a kind of ornate golden chair, like a throne. There were thin veils arranged in a canopy, a transparent tent obscuring the throne and the figure upon it. A giant golden statue of the Lord Buddha stood against the far wall.

Thomni and his Abbot stood before the throne. Both had the blank expressionless faces of men under deep hypnosis. Padmasambvha spoke. Even though he was now seated before them, his voice still seemed to come from everywhere and nowhere, filling the room. 'We are grateful for the return of our holy ghanta. The Doctor is our friend. Thomni, you will go to Khrisong. Tell him that the Abbot orders the Doctor's release.'

Thomni bowed. Still in the same trance-like state, he turned to leave. The voice spoke again. 'Remember, these words were spoken by the Abbot. You have never seen me or heard my voice. You have never entered this room.'

Thomni bowed again and left. He did not even notice when the doors of the Sanctum opened and closed behind him of their own accord.

In the Anteroom, Thomni seemed to wake up with a jerk. He gazed around him wildly. Then he remembered. He had been given a most important errand, by the Abbot Songtsen himself... Thomni ran from the room.

In the Sanctum, the voice of Padmasambvha was saying, 'We must make certain, Songtsen, that the Doctor learns nothing of what is happening here. He may not be in sympathy with the power that now guides us. He might even seek to hinder the Great Plan. It would be well if he were to depart as soon as possible.'

The Doctor was starting to feel cold and cramped as he hung in his bonds from the ring on the Monastery door. Khrisong and his warriors were cold and cramped too, waiting high on the walls. But they stood guard bravely, spears and bows ready to hand. Suddenly one of them turned excitedly to Khrisong. 'There – coming down the path. Three of them.'

Khrisong looked. 'Yes, I see them. Your eyes are keen, Rapalchan! Make ready, all of you!' Khrisong's archers fitted arrows to their bows. Others balanced spears, ready to hurl.

Nearby, on the mountain path, Jamie and Victoria had just seen the lights of the Monastery.

'There it is, Jamie. Look – there's the Doctor waiting for us by the door.' In her excitement, Victoria began to run ahead. Jamie ran to catch up with her. Travers, behind them, broke into a trot.

On the Monastery walls, Khrisong and his warriors waited, bows drawn and ready, watching the three figures running towards them in the darkness. 'The Yeti are coming, brothers,' whispered Khrisong exultantly. 'As soon as they are in bowshot – slay them! Kill them all!'

4

Jamie Traps a Yeti

The Doctor strained his eyes, trying to pick out the three shapes running down the mountain path towards him. For a moment the distance and the gloom misled him. Perhaps the Yeti really were coming to rescue him. He looked again, then chuckled to himself. Of course – Victoria and Jamie! And that looked very like Travers behind them.

Suddenly a terrifying thought struck the Doctor. If *he* could mistake the three for attacking Yeti, might not Khrisong and his warrior monks do the same? Tired, nervous men, bows and spears in their hands, waiting in the darkness to be attacked. They'd let fly at anything that moved!

Frantically the Doctor yelled, 'Victoria, Jamie, keep back. They'll kill you!'

On the mountainside Victoria could just hear the Doctor's voice, but the wind carried away his actual words. 'All right, Doctor, we're coming!' she cried, and ran even faster.

Up on the wall, a young monk panicked. Without waiting for Khrisong's order, he drew his bow and fired.

An arrow thudded into the snowy ground at Victoria's

feet. Jamie came up beside her. 'Look,' cried Victoria. 'They're shooting at us.'

Travers joined them and gazed in amazement at the arrow. 'Damn fools – what do they think they're doing?'

Khrisong meanwhile was leading a picked band of warriors down from the wall, and out of the main gate, ready to do battle with the Yeti. As Khrisong emerged, the Doctor called, 'Please! Don't shoot! Those are friends of mine.'

'We know that, Doctor,' shouted Khrisong, 'but your Yeti shall not rescue you!'

The Doctor strained at his bonds. 'They're not Yeti, man. They're hardly more than children.'

Khrisong ignored him. 'Ready, brothers?' The little band of monks prepared to shoot at the three figures on the path. Bows were drawn, spears raised in readiness. It was Travers who saved them all. Shouldering Jamie and Victoria aside, he ran straight at the little group of warriors, ignoring the danger. 'Stop all this nonsense at once – it's me, Travers. You know me!'

'Perhaps it is witchcraft,' one of them muttered. 'The Yeti try to trick us with their magic, speaking with the voice of Travers. Better to kill, and be sure.' He raised his spear.

Khrisong stopped him, knocking the spear aside. 'No. It is Travers!'

Travers puffed up to him angrily. 'Look here, what do you think you're doing?' he shouted.

Khrisong said, 'I am sorry. It was a mistake. Who are

these others?'

'Couple of kids I met on the mountain. Say they're friends of the Doctor's.' Travers called over to his two companions. 'It's all right, come down. It's safe now.'

Jamie and Victoria ran to the Doctor. Furiously, Jamie asked Khrisong, 'What's going on? Why's the Doctor tied up like that?'

'He is a suspected criminal,' said Khrisong sternly. 'So too are you, if you are his friends. Seize them!'

One of the monks tried to grab Victoria. Jamie promptly knocked him down, snatching away his spear. He turned threateningly on the approaching monks. Trouble seemed inevitable. Another monk ran out from inside the Monastery. It was Thomni. 'Wait, Khrisong,' he called. 'I have a message for you from the Abbot.'

Khrisong held up his hand to restrain the warriors. 'Well?'

'This man has brought back the sacred ghanta. We must treat him with all kindness and respect. Those are the commands of the Abbot.'

Khrisong swung round on the Doctor, 'Why did you not tell me of this?'

The Doctor smiled. 'Would you have listened?'

Khrisong glared at him for a moment, then nodded to one of the monks. The monk stepped forward and began cutting the Doctor's bonds. 'I'm sure the Abbot meant his words to apply to my friends as well,' said the Doctor mildly. The warriors menacing Jamie and Victoria stood back. Victoria ran to the Doctor. 'Are you

51

all right?' she said.

The Doctor rubbed his wrists. 'Oh, I think so. A little stiff, perhaps. They were using me as Yeti bait, you see! But there's no real harm done.' Looking sternly at Travers, the Doctor continued sternly, 'But there might have been, Mr Travers. We might all have been killed. All through that ridiculous story of yours. Isn't it time you told the truth?'

'What truth?' asked Khrisong sternly.

Travers looked thoroughly abashed. 'I'm sorry, Khrisong. I'm afraid I misled you. It couldn't have been the Doctor who attacked me. The thing was huge – not human at all. I just wanted him safely locked up. I didn't mean you to hurt him.' Khrisong turned in disgust and strode back inside the Monastery.

Thomni said apologetically, 'Doctor, the Abbot has given orders for comfortable quarters and refreshments to be prepared for you. Later, when you are rested, he would like to see you and thank you. Shall we go inside?'

The Doctor said, 'An excellent idea. Come along, you two. You come as well, Mr Travers. You may have got us into trouble but at least you helped to get us out.'

They all went back inside the Monastery and the great bronze doors clanged to behind them.

High on the mountainside, three enormous, shaggy shapes were standing motionless near the mouth of the cave where Jamie and Victoria had been trapped. Suddenly they jerked into life. As if in obedience to a common command, they began lumbering down the path, towards the Monastery.

In the simple guest room provided by the monks, the Doctor finished a mug of scalding Tibetan tea and sighed with pleasure. 'My thanks to your Abbot, Thomni. A truly splendid meal.' Jamie and Victoria exchanged glances.

'Och, yes,' muttered Jamie. 'It was verra nice.'

'Yes, it was lovely,' added Victoria.

Actually neither of them were very impressed with Tibetan food. The pile of yellow rice, covered with strange meats and vegetables, had been palatable enough, especially since they were both ravenous with hunger. But the milkless, unsweetened tea with Yak butter floating in it had been too much for them. Travers had eaten and drunk with gusto. Victoria supposed he must be used to strange foods. As for the Doctor, he seemed ready, as usual, to eat and drink anything, anywhere, with anyone.

Thomni flushed with pleasure at their praise. 'When you have rested further the Abbot will wish to see you and thank you, Doctor.' He bowed and withdrew. Travers poured the Doctor another mug of tea. 'You certainly seem to be well in with the monks, Doctor.'

The Doctor smiled. 'Well, it is my second visit, you know.'

'I thought I was one of the first white men to reach here,' said Travers. 'When *was* your first visit?'

'Oh, about three hundred years ago,' replied the

Doctor airily. Ignoring Travers' astonished reaction, he went on. 'Jamie, let's have another look at this sphere you found in the cave.' Jamie fished it out, and handed it over. The Doctor stared at it, lost in thought.

'I still don't believe those things that attacked us were my Yeti,' said Travers argumentatively. 'All the reports agree – the creature is shy and timid. The monks confirm it too. In the old days the Yeti were hardly ever seen.'

'Yet all at once they've become bold and savage,' said the Doctor thoughtfully. Travers nodded.

'According to the monks they've been killing all sorts of people, attacking the camps of the pilgrims and merchants, just as they did mine.'

'Maybe they don't want people to come here any more,' suggested Victoria.

'They, or whoever's controlling them,' chimed in Jamie. They all looked at him in surprise. Jamie felt suddenly embarrassed.

'Go on, Jamie,' said the Doctor encouragingly. He knew that although the Scots lad was more of a fighting man than a thinker, he had a shrewd, quick mind, especially where practical problems were concerned.

'I've been thinking, Doctor,' said Jamie. 'Yon beastie – there was something awful strange about it. What kind of an animal can get smashed over the head with a pile of rocks and scramble out as good as new? And the other one, by the TARDIS, it didna attack at all. I'm no' sure they're just animals at all. They're not *natural* somehow.'

The Doctor sighed. 'I'd like to see one of these things,

I really would.'

As if in answer to the Doctor's wish, Thomni rushed into the room. 'Mr Travers, Doctor, you must come at once. The Yeti are approaching the Monastery!'

Travers, Jamie and Victoria leaped to their feet and followed Thomni from the room. Before he left, the Doctor placed the silver sphere which Jamie had given him carefully on the bed, under the pillow. Then he followed the others.

In the torch-lit courtyard, there was a scene of bustle and activity. Khrisong had every available warrior monk armed, and on duty. Some were being sent to the observation platform, others waited by the doors in case the Yeti should try to break through.

The Doctor and his little party stood on an observation platform, looking out over the walls. It was dark now, and they could just make out the bulk of the mountain as it loomed over the Monastery. The area just before the gates was lit up by blazing torches on the walls, but beyond their circle of light, it was hard to see anything at all. 'Well, where are they?' grumbled Travers.

'Wait,' said Khrisong. 'When the moon comes from behind those clouds, you will see them. They are very close.' As he spoke the moon began to appear. Its rays lit up the snow-covered mountain, the track leading upwards. Then they saw them. A group of shaggy forms, milling about just beyond the circle of torch-light.

'That's them, right enough,' said Jamie. 'There's a whole gang of them now!'

Travers had a pair of battered binoculars to his eyes. His face was radiant. 'At last,' he was muttering. 'At last. Look at them! Aren't they magnificent?'

Victoria wasn't so enthusiastic. 'Doctor, look,' she whispered. 'They're coming nearer.' And, indeed, the lumbering figures seemed to be edging closer and closer to the Monastery gates.

The Doctor tapped Khrisong's shoulder. 'Do you think they'll attack?' Khrisong's face was grim.

'I cannot tell, Doctor. We can only be ready. But they have never come so close before.'

The Doctor had taken the binoculars from a reluctant Travers and was staring eagerly at the creatures. 'You know, Jamie, I see what you mean. There's something about the way they move...' He handed the binoculars back. 'Oh, I do wish I could examine one properly. Do you think you could capture one for me?'

Jamie chuckled. 'Oh, aye, nothing to it. Shall we wrap it up for you, Doctor?'

Khrisong looked at the Doctor in amazement. 'We will kill them, Doctor – if we can. But why should we wish to capture one?'

'Because *if* you can get me one to examine, I may be able to find out why the Yeti have suddenly become killers. I might even be able to find a way for you to defeat them.'

Jamie cleared his throat. 'You're really serious, Doctor? About needing one of those beasties?'

'Very much so, Jamie.'

'Och, well, I think I can get hold of one for you. I'll need some equipment, Khrisong, and the help of those warriors of yours.'

Khrisong looked dubiously at Jamie. 'You are little more than a boy...'

'Believe me, Khrisong,' said the Doctor firmly, 'if Jamie says he can do it – he can do it. I've seen him in some very tight corners indeed.'

Khrisong turned to Jamie. 'Well, boy, what do you need?'

'Come on, Victoria,' said the Doctor. 'I think we'd better get out of the way. It's time we paid our respects to the Abbot Songtsen.'

The Great Hall was the biggest room in the Monastery. It was filled with long tables and benches, enough to hold hundreds of monks when they gathered for food and prayer. Now only a handful of lamas were assembled.

'Do not fear, brethren,' Songtsen was saying, 'I am sure that the return of the sacred ghanta means better times for us at Det-sen.'

'Master Abbot,' Sapan objected mildly, 'even now the Yeti gather at our gates to attack us.'

The Abbot smiled reassuringly. 'Have faith. Khrisong and his warriors will protect us.'

Sapan frowned. 'Khrisong is a rash and angry man. He disobeyed me, Lord Abbot. So sure was he that the Doctor was a danger to us.'

There was a deprecating cough from the doorway. The

lamas looked up to see the Doctor and Victoria standing in the doorway. 'Me, a danger?' said the Doctor. 'I can assure you I'm not. In fact, I very much hope I can help you.'

The Abbot came forward, smiling. 'You have helped us greatly already, Doctor, by returning the sacred ghanta. We owe you much.'

In the Monastery courtyard, Jamie had taken charge of things with a will. Except for a few sentries, he had all the warrior monks, and Travers too, assembling a kind of improvised net. All the available ropes in the Monastery had been woven together into a sort of tangled cat's cradle. Khrisong looked on, half resentful and half amused, as Jamie harried the monks into doing exactly what he wanted. 'Och, no, ye great loon. The rope goes over *there*, and under *here*. Then tie it *there*. And make those knots good ones. If the beastie gets loose, we shall all be for it.'

At last the work was complete. The improvised net lay spread out in the courtyard, long ropes tied to each corner. Under Jamie's instructions, a party of monks carried the net out through the doors, and spread it on the ground just under the wall. 'Right,' said Jamie. 'Off you go, the lot of you.' The monks, all except for Thomni and Khrisong, went back inside. Jamie waited a moment then yelled, 'Ready inside?' He grabbed one of the long ropes attached to a corner, coiled it, and threw it over the wall. He did the same thing with the ropes at the other three corners of the improvised net. Quickly, Jamie dashed back inside the courtyard to check.

The ends of the four ropes were now dangling over the wall inside the courtyard. A couple of brawny young monks had hold of each rope. Travers was in charge of them. 'Remember,' said Jamie grimly, 'when you hear me yell "Now!", tug with all your might, and dinna let go.' Travers nodded determinedly, Jamie grabbed a flaming torch from the wall, and went outside where Khrisong and Thomni were waiting, both armed with heavy spears.

Jamie looked at the outspread net, the ropes at each corner stretching away over the wall. 'All we need now is a Yeti,' he said cheerfully. 'I'll just awa' and whistle one up!'

'You are brave, stranger,' said Thomni. 'Our prayers go with you.'

Holding his blazing torch in front of him, Jamie set off up the mountain path towards the waiting Yeti.

All this time the little group of Yeti had stayed on the mountain, sometimes advancing, sometimes retreating, but never far away. Jamie whistled to keep his spirits up as he came closer to them. He picked the nearest Yeti, and marched boldly towards it.

The Yeti stood motionless as he approached. Just like the one outside the TARDIS, thought Jamie. Even when he was almost within touching distance, the creature didn't move. Jamie held up his torch. The light glinted on the Yeti's yellow fangs, and was reflected fierily in its little red eyes. Jamie summoned up all his courage, and yelled at the top of his voice, 'Garn, ye great hairy loon. I'll have you for a doormat, so I will!' He thrust the flaming torchlight right under the Yeti's nose, close enough to singe its whiskers.

With a nerve-shattering roar the Yeti came to life. A giant, hairy hand aimed a savage slash at Jamie's head. Jamie ducked, turned, and ran back down the path at full speed. He could hear the angry howls of the Yeti as it lumbered after him.

He timed his speed carefully, letting the Yeti get as close as he could without actually being caught. He didn't want the beast to get discouraged and give up. Soon Jamie was nearly at the Monastery gates, where Khrisong and Thomni waited, spears in hand. Now if he could only lure the creature on to the net…

Jamie was almost there, when he slipped and fell on the icy ground. The Yeti loomed over him, the great clawed hands reaching out. Jamie, the breath knocked out of him, lay helpless on the ground.

Khrisong and Thomni ran forward, thrusting at the Yeti with their spears. The creature whirled round on them, shattering Thomni's spear at a single blow. Khrisong held it off alone, jabbing and thrusting with his spear while Thomni helped Jamie to his feet.

Khrisong fought hard, but his blows had no effect. He was forced to fall back before the attacking monster. The Yeti lumbered further and further forward. It advanced until it was standing right on the net. 'Khrisong, get back!' shouted Jamie. With a final spear-thrust Khrisong leaped backwards, and Jamie gave a mighty yell of 'Now!' at the top of his voice.

In the courtyard, Travers shouted 'Heave!' The warrior monks pulled hard on the ropes. The corner ropes jerked taut, and, caught in the net, the Yeti was lifted off its feet. It was slammed against the wall, then tugged higher and higher off the ground. The Yeti thrashed about frenziedly in the tangle of ropes, roaring with rage. More armed monks ran from the courtyard and began belabouring the Yeti with swords, spears and clubs. None of their blows had the slightest effect. The maddened creature still continued its thrashing and roaring. It ripped savagely at the net and, to his horror, Jamie saw some of the ropes beginning to fray and snap. To make matters worse, no one told the monks inside the courtyard to *stop* pulling. The entangled monster was jerked higher and higher up the wall, until it was out of reach of those attacking it from below.

'They'll pull it over the top and inside with them in a minute,' thought Jamie, 'and the beast's alive and kicking!'

He turned to go and warn the monks in the courtyard, when suddenly he saw that it was already too late. The net was coming apart like a wet paper bag. With the Yeti hanging almost at the top of the high wall, it flew to pieces. There was a tremendous thud as the Yeti slammed down on to the icy ground below, and lay completely still. Cautiously the ring of warrior monks approached

it. Khrisong jabbed it with his spear. The Yeti didn't stir. 'The thing is dead,' said Thomni.

Jamie nodded. 'It wasna just as I'd planned it, but it's worked out well enough. Come on. Let's get the puir beastie inside.'

As the monks began to drag the Yeti into the courtyard, Jamie turned and looked up the mountain path. The little group of Yeti stood motionless, watching. Then, moving with one accord, they turned and shambled into the darkness.

Jamie turned and followed the monks inside. One of the warrior monks began clearing up the remains of the broken net from the place where the Yeti had fallen. As he did so, his sandalled foot came down on a little silver sphere, pressing it down further into the icy mud.

In the Great Hall, the Yeti lay stretched out on the huge central dining table. The Hall was brightly lit, for the Doctor had called for extra torches. Outside waited a hushed group of monks and lamas. At first they had all crowded round the table, eager to see the captured Yeti. But the Doctor had chased them away, saying he couldn't work in the middle of a Rugby scrum. Only Travers, Jamie, Victoria, Khrisong and Thomni were allowed to stay.

The Doctor leaned over the prostrate Yeti. Victoria thought he looked rather like a surgeon at the operating table. She stood well at the back of the little group. She wasn't going to get too close to the Yeti, even if it was dead. Victoria and the Doctor had come running at the news of the Yeti's capture, and she had scolded Jamie for taking such terrible risks.

The Doctor looked up. 'Well, I can tell you one thing. This creature isn't flesh and blood. Look!' He beckoned them forward and indicated a place on the massive arm. He had removed a patch of fur. Beneath it they could see the unmistakable glint of metal. 'You were right – it's not your Abominable Snowman after all, Travers,' the Doctor added.

'Then what is it, Doctor?' Travers asked.

'It is witchcraft,' snarled Khrisong. 'The thing is a servant of the devil.'

The Doctor shook his head. 'Not quite. It's some kind of robot, I think.'

'No wonder we couldna kill it with spears,' said Jamie.

'The thing is,' said the Doctor, 'why did it stop working?' He returned to his examination.

'Maybe something inside it got broken in the fall?' suggested Victoria.

The Doctor was examining the fur on the creature's massive chest. 'Wait a moment,' he muttered. 'Jamie, lend me your knife.' Jamie slipped the dagger from his stocking, and passed it to the Doctor. Slipping the point into a crevice in the fur, the Doctor prised open a little trapdoor, revealing a hollow, empty space.

'There's nothing in there,' said Victoria.

'No, but there should be. When you trapped it, Jamie,

you must have dislodged its control unit. That's why it went dead.'

'So if it gets its control unit *back*,' said Jamie slowly, 'it could come to life?'

The Doctor nodded gravely. 'Yes, Jamie, I think it could.'

Outside the Monastery, the silver sphere embedded in the ground stirred feebly, trying to free itself. But the icy mud held it gripped fast. It began to pulse rhythmically, sending out some kind of signal.

In the Doctor's quarters, the little silver sphere came to life. It, too, pulsed with a signal. Then it rolled slowly from the bed, on to the floor and out of the room.

A kitchen monk came along the corridor, on his way to clear away the remains of the Doctor's meal. As he approached, the little sphere rolled into a dark corner. Once the monk had gone, the sphere resumed its journey, moving inch by inch towards its ultimate destination – the 'dead' Yeti on the table in the Great Hall. It had a long way to go. The Great Hall was in a distant part of the Monastery. But it would get there in the end.

5

The Secret of the Inner Sanctum

Hands deep in his pockets, the Doctor paced up and down the Great Hall. 'We've got to find that control unit. It's far too dangerous to be left around.'

Jamie nodded in vigorous agreement. 'You're telling me. We dinna want yon beastie coming to life again. Especially now we've brought it in here with us.'

'Exactly,' said the Doctor. 'Come on.' He set off briskly for the door, but the tall figure of Khrisong barred his way.

'Where are you going?' demanded Khrisong sternly.

The Doctor looked up at him impatiently. 'To have a look outside the gates.'

'No, I will not allow it.'

The Doctor sighed. 'My dear chap, why ever not?'

'You say someone made this creature and sent it against us? Why? Who wishes harm to the monks of Det-sen? I will trust no stranger until these questions are answered.'

Jamie glared at Khrisong furiously. 'Have we no' convinced you yet? We're on your side!'

'Khrisong,' said the Doctor patiently, 'why won't you let us help you?'

'I do not need your help. Thomni, guard these strangers well.' Khrisong turned and strode from the room.

The Doctor shook his head. 'My word, he's an obstinate fellow.'

Travers cleared his throat. 'Afraid you're right, Doctor. Still, that's it. Nothing more we can do. Think I'll get some sleep. Night everybody.' Travers bustled from the room, suddenly in a great hurry.

He ran along the corridor and out into the courtyard. Over by the closed and barred door, he could hear Khrisong talking to the sentry. 'No one is to leave the Monastery. And be watchful. The Yeti are even more dangerous than we feared. Send men to fasten with chains the one that we captured.' As Khrisong strode back across the courtyard, Travers intercepted him.

'Khrisong! I must talk to you.'

Khrisong paused reluctantly. 'Well?'

Travers' voice was low and urgent. 'We know now that the creatures who've been attacking you are robots. They're not the real Yeti at all. I've always said the Yeti were timid and harmless. You've got to let me go out and find their cave. Perhaps there may still be some real Yeti there. I *must* know. Otherwise the whole point of my expedition will be lost.'

'No. I will not allow anyone to leave.'

'You can't give *me* orders, you know,' said Travers truculently. '*I'm* not one of your monks.'

'I command here. And I say no one is to leave. Anyone may be controlling these monsters. Even you.'

68

Travers was about to argue further, then a sudden thought struck him. He glanced over at the sentry, not far away. 'Thank you, Khrisong, old chap. Thank you very much!' said Travers in a suddenly loud voice. He saw the sentry glance towards them.

'Why do you thank me?' snapped Khrisong.

Travers smiled. 'For making me see sense,' he said quietly. Then, raising his voice again, 'Well, thanks again. Good night.'

Khrisong stared at him as if he were mad, and strode away. Travers waited until he was out of sight, then walked quickly across to the sentry at the gate. 'I've just been having a word with Khrisong,' he said. 'He's given me permission to leave the Monastery.'

In the Great Hall, the Doctor was getting nowhere.

'I'm sorry, Doctor,' said Thomni firmly. 'I myself would trust you. But I must obey the orders of Khrisong.'

'I suppose you must,' said the Doctor sadly. He wandered back to the table where the Yeti lay stretched out.

'Doctor,' said Victoria timidly, 'that space you found in the Yeti's chest – it's round, isn't it?'

The Doctor nodded. 'That's right, my dear. Why do you ask?'

'Well,' said Victoria, 'that silver sphere thing we took from the cave… that was round, too. It would just about fit in that space.'

'Aye, so it would,' said Jamie excitedly. 'It could be one

of those control units too!'

The Doctor struck his forehead and groaned. 'I'm an idiot. An absolute imbecile. You're quite right, of course. Let's go and find it.'

Guided by a puzzled but helpful Thomni, they hurried down the endless corridors of the rambling old Monastery, on the way back to the Doctor's room. 'It's a good job you're with us,' gasped Victoria. 'This place is a real rabbit-warren.'

At the sound of their approaching feet in the corridor, the little silver sphere rolled swiftly under the base of a statue of Buddha which stood nearby. The Doctor and his party hurried past. Once they were gone, the sphere rolled from under the statue, and, hugging the darkest corners, moved slowly on its way.

In his room, the Doctor was rummaging frantically on his bed. 'I left it here, just under the pillow. I *know* I did!'

Victoria and Jamie joined in the search. 'Well, it's no' here now,' said Jamie when they had finished. 'Someone must have taken it.'

'Travers!' said Victoria suddenly. 'I thought it was odd, the way he rushed off.'

'It does seem a possibility,' agreed the Doctor. 'I hate to accuse anyone without proof – but perhaps we'd better ask him.'

'I will take you to his room,' said Thomni. 'It is next to yours.' He led them a little way along the corridor to a small bare room, much like the Doctor's. 'You see,' said

Victoria triumphantly. 'He's not here – and he said he was going to sleep.'

'We could search the place,' suggested Jamie.

The Doctor frowned. 'I don't think that would be any use. If he has taken it, he'll have it on him. We'll have to find him.'

'All verra well,' said Jamie, 'but where do we start in a place this size?'

The Doctor was already on his way to the door. 'At the main gate, I think. Since he isn't in his room, he's probably trying to leave the Monastery.'

After another dash along the corridors, they reached the courtyard. The Doctor rushed up to the sentry at the doors. 'Have you seen Mr Travers, by any chance?'

The sentry nodded. 'It was some time ago. He has gone now.'

'Gone?' snapped Thomni. 'Out of the Monastery?'

'Yes, Captain. He told me Khrisong had given his permission.'

'That is impossible. He has tricked you.'

Thomni turned to the Doctor. 'We must inform Khrisong of what has happened. He is with the Abbot Songtsen. Will you come with me, please?'

As they walked across the courtyard, the Doctor said thoughtfully, 'I still can't believe Travers has anything to do with controlling these robots. Or with taking the sphere come to that.'

Victoria looked at him affectionately. As usual, the Doctor was being far too trusting. He always found it

71

hard to think ill of anybody. 'Well, one thing's certain, Doctor,' she told him. 'That sphere couldn't have moved off on its own.' She had no idea that, in a corridor not far away, the little silver sphere was doing exactly that.

With the Abbot Songtsen at his side, Khrisong strode into the Great Hall. 'The monster is here, Lord Abbot. I have had it fastened down with chains...' Khrisong stopped short at the sight of Sapan and Rinchen. The two old lamas were building an elaborate framework of wood and coloured threads, which completely surrounded the prostrate body of the Yeti. 'What are you doing?' Khrisong asked impatiently.

The Abbot smiled. 'They are constructing a ghost trap, Khrisong. Is it not so, my brethren?'

Sapan nodded proudly. 'We have built a spirit trap about the monster, to restrain its evil, my Abbot.'

'It was well thought of,' said the Abbot gently. 'You are wise, Sapan.'

Khrisong laughed. 'I think my chains will be of more use,' he said. 'See, Lord Abbot.' Khrisong pointed to the heavy chains which now fastened the Yeti to the great stone table.

Offended, the two old lamas prepared to go. Sapan paused by the door. 'You should never have allowed this monster to be brought into the Monastery, Khrisong,' he reproved. And with this parting shot, he followed his friend down the corridor.

Khrisong shouted after him. 'What I allow is my

business, Sapan.'

Songtsen held up a restraining hand. 'Gently, my son.'

Khrisong looked rather ashamed of himself. 'I am sorry, my Abbot. Sapan and his fellow lamas find much fault in me of late.'

'Harsh words are like blunted arrows, my son. Only the truth can make them sharp.'

'I have only tried to do my duty, my Abbot. The protection of the Monastery is in my hands.'

'I know, Khrisong. Your task is not an easy one.'

Khrisong gazed down at the tethered Yeti. 'And such is our adversary. It is against these creatures that I must protect you. My life is nothing if I fail.' He gestured angrily towards the monster, still terrifying as it lay motionless. 'Can I combat *this* with mildness?'

'Our ways are the ways of peace, my son. You must not seek to change them.'

'I fight to preserve them, my Abbot. There is no other way.'

A strange, faraway expression came over the old Abbot's face. 'There is. It is merely obscured to our simple minds. I will seek guidance of our Master, Padmasambvha.' The Abbot sank cross-legged to the floor, in the classic position for meditation.

The Doctor rushed into the room, followed by Thomni, Jamie and Victoria. With a quick glance at Songtsen, who didn't appear even to see him, the Doctor said, 'Khrisong! Did you give Travers permission to leave the Monastery?'

'Of course not.'

'Well, he's awa',' said Jamie.

Briefly the Doctor explained what had happened.

Khrisong marched to the door. 'You will come with me, Doctor.' The Doctor looked pleased. 'Going to let me help at last, are you?'

'No, Doctor. I merely wish to make sure that you do not vanish also.' With that, Khrisong strode from the room, the Doctor and Jamie following him.

Victoria hung back for a word with Thomni. She rather liked the shy young warrior monk. She indicated the Abbot, still sitting motionless. 'Is he all right?'

'Oh yes,' whispered Thomni reverently. 'He is in a trance. We must leave him.'

Victoria jumped, as suddenly the old Abbot spoke, in a distant faraway voice. 'Yes, Master, I will obey. I come.' Moving like a sleep-walker, the Abbot rose and walked slowly from the room.

'Who was he talking to?' whispered Victoria.

Thomni's voice was hushed in awe. 'To our Master, Padmasambvha, in the Holy Sanctum.'

'Your Master? I thought the Abbot was in charge?'

'And so he is. But above him is the Most Holy Padmasambvha, who rules us all.'

'What's he like?' asked Victoria curiously.

'I do not know. I have never seen him.' Thomni believed he was speaking the truth – his visit to the Inner Sanctum had been wiped from his mind.

'How long has he been here?'

Thomni shrugged. 'Forever, perhaps. He is ageless.'

A look of mischief came over Victoria's face. 'Can't we go to this Sanctum place, and take a peep at him?'

Thomni was appalled. 'Most certainly not. Only the Abbot may enter the Sanctum.'

'Don't you want to know what your Master looks like? Surely you do?'

Thomni was firm. 'No, I do not. It is forbidden, and I have been brought up in the path of obedience. Now, Victoria, I think I must take you to your room. You will be safe there, till your friends return to look after you.'

Victoria sighed to herself, as Thomni marched her off. He was very nice, but he really was rather a stick-in-the-mud. Path of obedience, indeed. Victoria had her own ideas about that. But for the moment she said nothing. Smiling meekly at Thomni she followed him down the corridor.

At the main gate the unfortunate sentry was wishing he had never been born. 'But I saw you speak to him, Khrisong. I heard him thank you. Naturally, I thought...'

'You are a fool,' snapped Khrisong.

'Well, what's done is done,' interrupted the Doctor 'The important thing is that we examine a control unit. The one Jamie brought down from the mountains has vanished.'

'Aye, that's right,' Jamie joined in. 'So you've got to let

us go outside and look for the other one – the one that fell from the Yeti when we trapped it. It canna be far.'

For a long moment, Khrisong stood silent, considering. Then he nodded. 'Very well.' Jamie sighed with relief, and made for the doors. Khrisong held up a forbidding hand. 'No. *I* will go.'

Jamie watched resentfully, as the sentry opened the doors just enough for Khrisong to slip out into the night.

'Never mind, Jamie,' said the Doctor consolingly. 'At least *someone's* looking for the thing.'

Not far away, in the hush of the Inner Sanctum, Padmasambvha sat brooding. There was a small table just before him, the kind that might have been used to hold a chessboard. On it there stood instead a kind of model landscape – a relief-map of the Monastery, the mountain, and all the surrounding terrain. Little figures stood on the map, models of the Yeti, each about three inches high. Padmasambvha stretched out a withered, claw-like hand. For a moment, the hand hovered over the board, as the old Master focused the power of his will on the symbolic map. Then the hand picked up first one and then another of the Yeti models, and moved them from a position on the lower slopes of the mountain to one very close to the Monastery doors.

Out on the cold, dark mountainside two Yeti were standing. At the precise moment that Padmasambvha's withered hand moved their model counterparts, the two

Yeti began lumbering towards the Monastery.

Crouched behind a nearby boulder, a dark shape stirred. Travers watched as the two Yeti moved away. He was shivering with a mixture of excitement and terror. He got up, and continued his journey up the mountain.

Padmasambvha looked up from the board. The Abbot Songtsen was beside him, eyes glazed and face blank, held in a trance by the force of his Master's will. 'The Doctor is wise,' said Padmasambvha softly. 'His eyes are not closed in ignorance. But his mind is too complex. I cannot control it, as I control yours, Songtsen.' There was a hint of something cold and gloating in the thin, old voice. It was as though something else, some other being, spoke through the old monk's mouth.

'I must make sure that the Great Plan is imperilled no further.'

Again the withered hand stretched out and moved the two Yeti. This time they were almost at the Monastery doors.

In the circle of torchlight outside the Monastery doors Khrisong continued his search, unaware of the two giant, shaggy forms moving closer and closer.

6

A Yeti Comes to Life!

The Doctor and Jamie peered anxiously out of the Monastery door. In the torchlight they could see Khrisong, methodically searching the trampled ground in the area where the Yeti had fallen.

'Khrisong,' called the Doctor. 'Why don't you let us come out and give you a hand?'

'No!' Khrisong shouted back. 'You will stay where you are.' The sentry raised his spear, barring their exit.

Suddenly, Khrisong stooped down. At his feet was something that looked like a large pebble. But surely it was *too* round, *too* smooth? He prised it from the icy mud, and scraped it clean. Suddenly the sphere glowed in his hand, and emitted a high-pitched note. Khrisong jumped back, dropping the sphere in amazement.

The sphere gave out a second high-pitched note. As if in response to a signal, two Yeti loomed out of the darkness.

From the gateway, the Doctor shouted a warning. 'Khrisong! Look out! Yeti!' Khrisong looked up to see the two giant shapes bearing down on him. He backed away in horror. Then suddenly he stopped, holding his ground. The Yeti came menacingly on.

'Leave it, Khrisong!' the Doctor shouted. 'Come back in, you don't stand a chance.'

But in an act of lunatic courage, Khrisong dashed forward, snatching up the sphere from under the Yeti's feet. He turned to run for the doors, only to find the second Yeti barring his way. With terrifying speed a massive paw shot out and grabbed his wrist. Khrisong was a big, heavy man, but the Yeti held him dangling in the air, like a doll in the hand of a careless child. Khrisong screamed with pain, twisting and thrashing about, but he was utterly helpless.

Jamie snatched the spear from the sentry's grasp, and ran out of the gates. A shout from the Doctor summoned more warrior monks, and they too ran out to the rescue. Led by Jamie, the warriors began to rain blows upon the two Yeti, who responded with savage roars and slashing blows. The one holding Khrisong wrenched the sphere from his hand, and threw him to the ground like a discarded toy. Ignoring the attacking warriors, the two Yeti turned and disappeared into the darkness.

The Doctor and Jamie half-dragged, half-carried Khrisong back through the Monastery gates.

'Inside, all of you,' the Doctor yelled to the warrior monks. 'Don't follow them. You can't hurt them, you'll just get killed for nothing.'

Soon everyone was back inside and the doors were barred once more.

The Doctor and Jamie lowered the burly Khrisong to the ground. 'Is he all right?' asked Jamie. Before the

Doctor could reply, Khrisong struggled angrily to his feet.

'Of course I'm all right, boy,' he growled, rubbing his brawny arm. The Doctor examined it – the marks of the Yeti's paws could be seen, clearly embedded in the flesh.

'Just a little bruising,' the Doctor said. 'You're lucky you weren't killed.'

'Aye,' Jamie agreed. 'That was the daftest thing I ever saw – and the bravest.'

Khrisong ignored this. He looked at the Doctor in puzzlement. 'Why did they just leave? They had us at their mercy.'

'Because they got what they came for, I imagine. They didn't *want* to fight, they were after that control unit.'

Khrisong frowned. 'You speak as though these monsters were intelligent, Doctor.'

'They're being controlled,' explained the Doctor. 'Somehow that sphere was important to them. They *had* to get it back.'

'Did ye hear the screech it gave?' demanded Jamie.

'Some kind of signal – and that's a help. With the right kind of equipment, signals can be traced.'

'You have such equipment?' asked Khrisong.

'Yes, but not here, I'm afraid.' The Doctor looked significantly at Jamie. 'I'm afraid we've got to get back to the TARDIS.' Turning to Khrisong he explained. 'All my equipment is in my, er, camp, some way up the mountainside.'

'Then you must fetch it at once,' declared Khrisong.

Jamie looked at him in amazement. 'You're letting us go? Just like that?'

Khrisong looked a very shaken man, as he answered. 'I have no choice. My warriors are powerless. I *must* trust you, Doctor.'

'We'll try not to let you down,' said the Doctor. 'Let's just get our coats, Jamie, and we'll be on our way.'

They ran back to their rooms and struggled into warm clothing. There was no sign of Victoria. 'Probably wandering around somewhere,' said Jamie. 'Maybe it's better if she doesna know where we're going. She'd only worry.' With the Doctor in his huge fur coat, and Jamie in his anorak, they returned to the courtyard. Khrisong was waiting by the gate.

'Good fortune go with you,' he murmured gruffly. At Khrisong's signal the door was unbarred and opened, and Jamie and the Doctor slipped out into the night. Khrisong said to the sentry, 'Let no one pass. Call me if there is news. I shall be in my quarters.'

Padmasambvha looked up from his board. 'The Yeti have accomplished their task. Now I have a task for you, Songtsen.' The old Master held out his hand. In it was a small transparent pyramid. It seemed to glow with a sort of inner fire, as though there was a kind of life within it. Padmasambvha gestured towards the board, where three of the little Yeti models were grouped together. 'These three Yeti are waiting to escort you. Take this pyramid, which I have prepared, to the cave. Then, the

Great Intelligence will have its focus on this planet. Its wanderings in space will be over, and my task will be done. Go now, Songtsen!'

The Abbot bowed, took the strangely glowing pyramid, and left the Sanctum. Once again the doors opened and closed behind him of their own accord.

The Abbot glided along the corridors of the Monastery, and crossed the courtyard to the main gate. Surprised to see his Abbot, the sentry bowed. As the man straightened up, Songtsen passed a hand lightly across his face. Immediately the sentry stood motionless, waiting. In a quiet, faraway voice, Songtsen said, 'You will open the doors and let me pass. You will close them behind me. You will remember nothing.'

The sentry moved at once to the doors and opened them. The Abbot passed through. The sentry closed and barred the doors again. For a brief moment he stood motionless again. Then he seemed to wake with a start. He looked round, reassured to see that all was quiet and normal.

'Must have dozed off,' he thought. 'Lucky Khrisong wasn't around.' Confident that all was well, he resumed his watch.

The Doctor and Jamie trudged wearily up the mountain path, neither of them feeling very happy.

They were doing their best to keep a look-out in all directions at once. A cold wind howled round them. The moon kept drifting in and out of black clouds, so that they were alternately plunged in pitch darkness, or bathed in sinister, ghostly moonlight. Their footsteps sounded very loud as they crunched through the frozen snow. Every now and again, Jamie thought he could hear someone behind them, but when he stopped to listen the sound had gone. 'Och, I'm just getting jumpy,' he thought. 'And no wonder. Surely we're getting near the TARDIS by now?'

The Doctor came to a sudden halt. 'Jamie, look!' A little way ahead, just off the main path, stood the still forms of three Yeti. 'They're not moving,' whispered the Doctor. 'Maybe they're switched off. If I could just examine…'

Jamie tugged at his arm. 'Aye, and what if someone switches them on while you're doing it? Come on, let's get to the TARDIS while we still can.'

The Doctor sighed. 'I suppose you're right.'

The two moved off, looking back at the three Yeti until a turn in the path hid them from sight.

The three Yeti stood in the same spot, completely motionless.

After a few minutes the Abbot Songtsen came softly up the path. His sandalled feet made almost no sound, and in spite of his thin robes he didn't appear to feel the biting cold. With the same gliding, sleep-walking motion he went up to the three Yeti.

He held out the glowing pyramid in his palms. The Yeti jerked into life. They formed themselves round him in a kind of hollow triangle. With his three strange escorts surrounding him, the Abbot Songtsen struck off away from the main path, heading for the cave of the Yeti.

Bored, and a little frightened, Victoria wandered round the echoing corridors. The Monastery seemed to be almost empty. She had looked in dormitory after dormitory, all deserted. She remembered Thomni telling her that most of the monks had been sent to other Monasteries for safety. She had wandered along corridors, down dusty staircases and through echoing halls, all now confused and identical in her mind.

Bored with waiting in her room, she had decided to go and hunt for the mysterious Inner Sanctum. Almost immediately she had become lost. She had long ago abandoned her plan to look for Padmasambvha, and would have been happy to settle for finding her own room again. Suddenly she saw a gleam of light ahead. She ran forward and found herself at the entrance to the Great Hall. Happy to be back on familiar ground, she crept inside.

The huge room was empty, except for the giant bulk of the Yeti stretched out on the table at the far end. Victoria walked towards it, half-fearful, half-fascinated. She looked in puzzlement at the complicated arrangement of wood and coloured threads surrounding it, and with relief at the chains that fastened it to the table.

As she was about to leave, she saw something silvery moving at her feet. It was the little silver sphere that

Jamie had brought from the mountain. She bent down and picked it up. 'Now how did you get all the way over here?' she said. As she glanced at the stretched-out Yeti, she saw the empty cavity that the Doctor had found in its chest. The little sphere would just fit inside, she thought. Victoria's hand began to stretch out towards the Yeti, and the sphere pulsed with light, and gave out a high-pitched signal. Victoria felt as though the sphere was moving her hand, rather than she the sphere.

Before she knew what was happening, she had slipped the silver ball into the little space on the Yeti's chest. The cavity snapped shut, and Victoria pulled back her hand.

For a moment nothing happened. Then the little red eyes of the Yeti snapped open. It began thrashing about in its bonds, shattering Sapan's spirit trap to pieces. To her horror, Victoria saw that the heavy chains were snapping almost as easily as the coloured threads of the ghost trap. In a matter of minutes the Yeti would be free!

7

A Plan to Conquer Earth

Not for the first time, Victoria's well-developed lungs came to her rescue. Too frightened to move, she let out a series of ear-splitting screams that echoed through every corridor of the Monastery. Warriors and lamas came running from every direction.

Thomni was first into the Great Hall, dashing in just as the Yeti broke through the last of its chains, and started making for Victoria. He grabbed the frightened girl, and bundled her into the corridor. 'Run, Victoria, run. Fetch Khrisong!'

As Victoria ran down the corridor, Thomni grabbed a heavy bronze incense-holder, almost as tall as himself, and prepared to use it as a club. He smashed it down on the Yeti's head. The blow landed with a tremendous impact that jarred Thomni's arms. He swung back the incense-holder for a second blow, but the Yeti roared angrily, and wrenched it from his grasp. Grasping the heavy metal pillar in both paws, the Yeti twisted it in two like a wax candle. Then it slashed out at Thomni. The glancing blow sent him spinning across the room and he crashed into a stone pillar. Ignoring him, the Yeti made for the doorway.

Thomni's attack had delayed it long enough to allow a little group of warrior monks to arrive. The Yeti burst through them, its sweeping blows smashing men to one side and the other. Several of the warriors struck at the monster with swords or spears, but the Yeti didn't even pause. Leaving a pile of wounded and bleeding warriors behind it, it shambled purposefully down the corridor.

As Victoria reached the courtyard she met Khrisong, and the main body of the warriors. Khrisong gripped her wrists fiercely.

'What has happened? Why are you screaming?'

'The Yeti, Khrisong! It's alive. It's broken free.'

Khrisong stared at her in disbelief. 'It's true,' she screamed. 'It's all my fault – I put back the sphere...'

Suddenly the Yeti appeared from the cloisters, and began moving towards the barred main doors. Khrisong smiled in grim satisfaction. 'This time we shall destroy it. Attack!'

Victoria crouched sobbing in a corner as Khrisong and his warriors fought their gallant and useless battle. The Yeti seemed almost uninterested in its human opponents. It simply continued its progress towards the main doors. Bowman after bowman loosed his arrows at point-blank range. Arrows thudded into the Yeti's hide until it looked like a porcupine. They didn't have the slightest effect. Savage blows from spears, swords, even axes simply rebounded from the monster's body. Whenever a rash warrior got too close, a single smashing blow from the Yeti put him out of the fight.

Victoria saw Thomni stagger into the courtyard, his face covered with blood. 'You've got to stop them,' she sobbed. 'They'll all be killed. They can't hurt it. It isn't alive. It's a robot.'

Thomni watched the useless battle for a moment, and saw that she was right. Running to the main doors, he unbarred them, and flung them wide. Immediately the Yeti began heading towards them. 'Close the doors,' yelled Khrisong furiously. 'We *must* destroy it.'

'No, brothers,' called Thomni. 'Let it go, or it will kill us all.'

Hurling aside the warriors in its way, the Yeti lumbered through the open doors and out into the night. Thomni, helped by some of the other monks, slammed the doors shut after it, and collapsed against them, panting for breath! All around, the courtyard was a shambles of dead and wounded men.

Dawn was breaking, as the Doctor and Jamie toiled up the mountain path on the last stages of their journey to the TARDIS. It was a beautiful and spectacular sight to see the sun rising over the snow-covered peaks, but they were both too tired and apprehensive to appreciate it properly.

The Doctor stopped for a moment, resting his back against a boulder. He huddled inside his big fur coat, gazing round the bleak terrain.

Jamie toiled up the path and leaned beside him, panting a little. Although the Doctor was small in stature, he seemed to have limitless resources of energy and strength. It was Jamie who was feeling the effects of the journey most. 'What's the matter, Doctor?' he asked, stamping his feet to bring back some feeling. His breath came out in little steamy puffs in the cold, clear morning air.

The Doctor gazed around abstractedly. 'Nothing, Jamie. Just taking a breather.'

Jamie looked at him, puzzled. The Doctor's head was cocked, like a hunting dog.

'You've heard something?'

'No. Nothing.'

'Let's be getting on then.'

The Doctor held up his hand. 'Just a moment. Something's worrying me.'

'I canna hear or see anything,' said Jamie, exasperatedly.

'Exactly. That's what's so worrying. It's all too quiet. Not a sign of the Yeti since we saw those three back there.'

'Aye, well, let's just be grateful, and get on to the TARDIS.'

As they set off again, the Doctor muttered, 'I still don't like it. There's something happening on this mountain. Something evil. I can feel it.'

Jamie looked round and shivered. 'Och, come on, will you? You're giving me the willies.'

Still further up the mountain, Travers was keeping watch on the cave of the Yeti. At least, he hoped it was their cave. On the journey to the Monastery, after he had first met Jamie and Victoria, he had made Jamie give him a detailed description of the cave and how to find it. Now he had been forced to wait until daylight to locate the place, and for hours he had been crouched in hiding, hoping desperately that it was the right cave.

He looked again at the huge boulder, standing in the cave mouth as a kind of door. It *must* be the place. Despite the cold and his lack of sleep, his fanatical enthusiasm kept him bright and alert.

He ducked further into cover. Two Yeti were moving towards the cave. One of them held something in its paw. As the Yeti came closer, Travers could just make out that it was holding a glowing silver sphere. The Yeti came up to the cave entrance, and then stopped. They made no attempt to move the boulder but simply stood like sentries, one each side of the door. Obviously they were waiting for something. But what? Travers studied them eagerly. Could they *all* be robots, as the Doctor said? Were there perhaps *real* Yeti, somewhere inside the cave? Travers settled down to wait.

Rounding a turn in the steep mountain path, the Doctor and Jamie came in sight of the rocky ledge where stood the TARDIS. A Yeti was standing beside it. Immediately, they moved back into cover.

'I said we'd been too lucky,' whispered the Doctor.

'What now?' asked Jamie.

The Doctor frowned ferociously. 'We've jolly well got

to get in to the TARDIS.'

Jamie was aghast at the unfairness of it all. 'What's the thing *doing* there? It can't have known we'd turn up.'

'It's just a robot, Jamie. It merely follows instructions. Now – I wonder...'

Suddenly, the Doctor stepped out of cover and into plain sight of the Yeti.

'Come back,' hissed Jamie. The Doctor ignored him, and walked closer to the monster. Nothing happened. Nothing at all. The Yeti just stood there, motionless. Cautiously, Jamie joined the Doctor, who turned and beamed at him.

'Do you know, Jamie, I think I know how to deal with it? I shall arrange a test!'

Jamie looked at him with respect. Trust the Doctor to come up with one of his brilliant scientific plans. 'What are you going to do?' he asked.

The Doctor chuckled. 'Bung a rock at it.' To Jamie's horror, the Doctor grabbed a rock from the ground and did just that. The rock whizzed through the air and bounced off the Yeti's nose. It still didn't react.

'Just as I thought. Can't see, can't hear, can't feel. Completely de-activated. Come on.' The Doctor marched right up to the Yeti and examined it at close range. He prodded it gently. 'Still, we'd better make sure. Lend me your knife, Jamie.'

Jamie was appalled. 'Dinna be so daft, Doctor. You might switch it on by mistake.'

'Oh, I don't think so. Just the opposite, I hope.'

Taking the little dagger, the Doctor probed the Yeti's chest, just as he'd done with the captured one at the Monastery. After a little fumbling, he prised open the chest cavity, revealing the little silver sphere. The Doctor reached in, and slowly and carefully removed it. With a sigh of relief he tossed the sphere to Jamie, and they moved towards the TARDIS.

'It's a wonder there wasn't some kind of protective mechanism,' said the Doctor thoughtfully. 'You'd think whoever built it would have thought of that!'

Jamie laughed. 'How many people do you think would go up to yon beastie, and start poking it with a wee dagger? The thing is, Doctor, they just didna reckon on anyone as daft as you!'

The Doctor gave him a mock-offended look, and opened the door of the TARDIS.

'How about some breakfast?' he suggested cheerily.

Outside the cave of the Yeti, Travers' long vigil was at last rewarded. He saw a group of shaggy figures moving across the mountainside towards him. Three more Yeti. Travers' eyes widened in amazement. In the centre of the little group of Yeti walked the Abbot Songtsen.

Songtsen marched up to the boulder outside the cave. He took the sphere from the Yeti holding it. The other Yeti lifted the enormous boulder aside and Songtsen entered the cave. The Yeti grouped themselves around the entrance, motionless once more.

*

In the Inner Sanctum the prayer lamps flickered, casting shadows in the gloom. The Master Padmasambvha was communing with the alien power that had dominated his being for so many weary years.

'Oh, Great Intelligence, the time for your Experiment has come at last. Abbot Songtsen makes the final preparations now. I ask only that you release me, as you have promised.' He sank back on the golden throne in infinite weariness.

The Abbot Songtsen was indeed busy about his preparations. Obeying the orders placed in his mind by Padmasambvha, who was himself performing the wishes of the Great Intelligence they both served, Songtsen was arranging the glowing spheres that Jamie had found into an intricate pattern. When the design was complete, Songtsen placed the pyramid given him by Padmasambvha reverently in the centre. Then he turned and walked from the cave. The pyramid began to pulse and flicker with life. Then, slowly, but surely, it began to grow…

Outside, Travers watched as Songtsen emerged. The Abbot set off down the mountain path. All the Yeti followed him.

Travers could scarcely believe his good fortune. The Yeti were gone, and the boulder at the mouth of the cave had not been replaced. He crept forward slowly, and entered the cave.

It was just as Jamie had described it – the pit-props,

the tunnel, and, in the distance, a glowing pulsating light. Jamie had not said how fierce and bright it was. And there was a kind of high-pitched noise… Eagerly, Travers crept up to the entrance of the inner cave. He looked through, and then fell back, shielding his eyes. In the centre of the pattern of spheres, the pyramid was pulsing and glowing, blazing with light. A high-pitched screaming sound filled the cave. It seemed full of a kind of exultant madness. Travers could feel it affecting his mind…

As Travers watched, the swollen pyramid cracked open. A bubbling, glutinous substance, shot with fiery colours, began to ooze forth. More and more of it poured forth, and then more and more still. It spread across the cave floor in a heavy mass, trickling slowly towards him. And it was still coming, far more than the pyramid could possibly hold! The thought flashed through Travers' confused mind that the pyramid was really a sort of gateway, a channel between some other, alien universe and this one. And that the other universe was pouring this evil substance through to this one. Pouring and pouring and pouring endlessly. Soon it would envelop the whole world…

With a mighty effort, Travers wrenched himself away. Half-demented, he ran from the cave, out through the tunnel and on to the mountainside. He began to run madly downwards, stumbling, falling, rising, and stumbling on, ignoring his hurts and bruises. He had to get away, away from the horror in the cave. What Travers found really unbearable about the heaving, bubbling mass, was the fact that he felt it was *alive*.

Jamie was happily spooning down the last of an enormous bowl of well-salted porridge. The Doctor was polishing off a plate of bacon and eggs. Somewhere in the TARDIS there was a machine that could produce any kind of food you could think of, piping hot and in a matter of seconds. Jamie had never been more glad of it. 'Och, that's better,' he said, pushing aside his bowl. 'But hadn't we better be getting back, Doctor?' The Doctor nodded, his mouth too full to speak. Wrapping themselves up for the outside, they prepared to leave.

'Mustn't forget this,' said the Doctor, picking up a little black box, covered with dials. 'My tracking device.'

Jamie picked up the sphere they had taken from the Yeti. 'What about this?'

'Oh, bring it along. I'll study it back at the Monastery.' They left the TARDIS, and the Doctor locked it behind them. The de-activated Yeti still stood motionless in the snow. The Doctor gave it an affectionate pat. 'Come on, Jamie,' he said, and set off down the mountain. Suddenly, he realised that Jamie wasn't following him. 'Come on, Jamie,' he repeated.

Jamie's voice was desperate. 'I canna, Doctor. I just canna. It's pulling me towards it.'

Turning, the Doctor saw Jamie. The sphere in his outstretched hand was being dragged by some invisible force closer and closer to the Yeti. The sphere was pulsing and glowing, emitting a high-pitched signal.

'Don't put it back,' yelled the Doctor. 'Whatever you do, don't put it back!' He rushed up to Jamie, grabbed him by the waist and tried to pull him away from the Yeti. But the invisible force exerted by the glowing sphere was more than a match for both of them. Step by step, Jamie and the Doctor were pulled closer and closer to the waiting Yeti.

'It's no good,' gasped Jamie. 'I'll have to let it go.'

'No, Jamie, you mustn't. You've *got* to hold on.' Letting go of Jamie's waist, the Doctor moved round in front of him. Just as the sphere slipped from Jamie's hands, he interposed his own body between the sphere and the Yeti. It thudded into the Doctor's ribs with painful force, ramming him back against the monster's body. The Doctor found he couldn't move. The pressure on his ribs increased. It seemed obvious that the sphere was determined to get back to the Yeti, even if it had to drill a hole through the Doctor to do it!

Jamie tried to move the sphere away from the Doctor, but he couldn't budge it. Painfully, the Doctor gasped, 'Jamie… get rock…'

'What's that, Doctor – I dinna understand.'

The pressure on the Doctor's ribs was now agonising. 'Find rock,' he sobbed. 'Same size… put in chest…'

All at once, Jamie saw what the Doctor meant. He abandoned his attempt to move the sphere, and groped round frantically for a suitably sized rock. All the stones around seemed too big or too small. He scrabbled frantically in the icy mud and snow, the sound of the

Doctor gasping for breath in his ears. At last, he saw a rock the same size and shape as the silver sphere. It was half buried in ice, and he couldn't shift it. Jamie kicked frantically at the rock with his boot heel. As soon as it came free, he dashed across to the Yeti and rammed it into the hole in the Yeti's chest.

Immediately, the pressure from the sphere cut off. It dropped harmlessly into Jamie's cupped hands.

The Doctor drew a deep, sobbing breath, and rubbed his aching chest. 'Are you all right?' asked Jamie anxiously.

'Just a bit breathless,' said the Doctor. 'No, don't do that – we may need it.' Jamie had drawn back his arm like a shot-putter, and was about to send the sphere whizzing over the horizon.

'But the thing nearly killed you, Doctor.'

'Not on purpose, though – it's simply programmed to return to… oh, my word!' The Doctor broke off as a sudden thought struck him.

It struck Jamie at the same time. 'The one back in the Monastery – maybe Travers didna take it!'

'Exactly,' agreed the Doctor. 'Victoria said it couldn't move by itself – but it can!'

'Aye,' said Jamie, 'and if it finds its way back to that Yeti we captured… we've got to warn them!'

Unaware that the catastrophe they feared had already happened, Jamie and the Doctor set off down the mountainside.

8

Revolt in the Monastery

The Monastery courtyard still showed the after-effects of battle. Injured monks were having their wounds dressed and bandaged. The dead were being carried away on stretchers, their faces covered.

Victoria finished bathing Thomni's forehead. 'There,' she said. 'That's better.' The young monk's face had been covered with blood, but most of it came from a long, shallow cut on his forehead. To Victoria's relief the injury wasn't nearly so bad as it looked. She was wringing out the cloth in a stone basin when Khrisong appeared. He glared furiously down at Thomni. 'Why did you disobey my orders?' he demanded.

Thomni tried to stand. He reeled dizzily, and had to hold on to Victoria. Gathering his strength, he replied, 'Because it was the only thing to do.'

'Had you not opened the gate,' growled Khrisong, 'the creature would not have escaped.'

Victoria came to Thomni's defence. 'If he hadn't opened the gate, you'd have *all* been dead by now,' she said spiritedly.

Khrisong rounded on her. 'And you – did you not say it was all *your* fault. What did you mean by that?'

Victoria was silent, staring at the ground.

'You'd better answer, Victoria,' said Thomni gently.

Without looking up, Victoria said, 'I put the control unit back in the Yeti. That's what brought it to life again.'

Khrisong called over two of his warriors. 'Seize her. Put her in the cell.'

'You don't understand,' sobbed Victoria. 'I didn't mean to do it. The sphere *made* me.'

'Spare her, Khrisong,' urged Thomni. 'She would not deliberately harm us. She must surely have been bewitched.'

Baffled and angry, Khrisong glared from one to the other. 'You are much of one mind, are you not? You disobey my orders, and she defends you. She confesses her crime, and you speak for her. Do you plot against me?'

'This is madness,' protested Thomni. But Khrisong was not listening.

'Take them both,' he ordered. 'Lock them up together. Let them do their plotting behind bars.'

Angrily he strode away across the courtyard, while the warrior monks closed in on Thomni and Victoria.

The Doctor and Jamie were trudging on down the mountainside, the Doctor carrying his detection device, Jamie gingerly carrying the silver sphere. Much to his relief, the sphere had stopped its signalling once they were away from the immobilised Yeti. 'The number of

102

times we've traipsed up and down this mountain...' Jamie was grumbling. Then he broke off short. The sphere had started its high-pitched signalling note again. 'Hey, Doctor,' he called. 'It's away again.'

The Doctor listened intently. 'That's a different sort of signal,' he said thoughtfully. 'Slightly different pitch.' He held his detection device close to the sphere, and studied the flickering dials intently.

Not far away the Abbot Songtsen and his escort of three Yeti were descending the mountain by a different route. Suddenly, the Yeti stopped. They paused as if listening, then, moving as one, they changed direction, setting off on a course which took them towards the Doctor and Jamie. The Abbot Songtsen, apparently unaware of what was happening, continued his journey down the mountain alone.

The Doctor peered excitedly at the flickering dials. 'You know, Jamie,' he said happily, 'I think I picked up some kind of answering signal! Isn't that splendid?'

Jamie was less enthusiastic. 'Can we no' just get back to the Monastery?' he asked plaintively. 'You can do all your detecting behind those nice high walls. So come on, will you?' And he set off down the mountain.

Obediently, the Doctor followed him. 'The trouble with you is, Jamie,' he said reproachfully, 'you lack the proper scientific spirit. This is a perfect opportunity to try and trace the main transmitter.'

'Aye,' said Jamie. 'And it's a perfect opportunity to get ourselves killed. While you're fiddling away with that machine, this thing's probably calling up all the Yeti in creation.'

For a while they plodded on in silence. The signal from the sphere stopped. Jamie began to hope they might reach the Monastery safely after all. Then, suddenly, the signal started up again. 'I wish you'd keep quiet,' muttered Jamie. He tried to muffle the sphere inside his anorak. 'Can we no' just throw it away, Doctor?'

'Too late for that, I'm afraid,' said the Doctor ruefully. 'Look!' Barring the path ahead, there stood three of the Yeti.

'We could maybe double back,' said Jamie. But when he looked over his shoulder, he saw that two more Yeti were blocking the path behind them. They were trapped.

For a long moment nobody moved. Then the Doctor said quietly, 'Jamie, give me the sphere. You take the detection device.' Quickly they made the exchange.

'Now what?' asked Jamie.

'We move forward. Very slowly.'

As they moved, the Yeti moved too, closing in on them.

The Doctor whispered urgently, 'When I say run, you run like the wind. Don't stop, and don't worry about me.'

'Och, no, Doctor—' protested Jamie.

The Doctor held up his hand. 'Please, Jamie, just run. Don't try to do anything heroic. Promise?'

'Aye, verra well.' By now they were almost up to the

three Yeti in front of them.

'Run, Jamie, run!' yelled the Doctor. Jamie sprinted down the path, dodging between the three Yeti like a centre-forward making for goal. They ignored him, and continued their advance on the Doctor. When they were almost within touching distance, the Doctor twisted round and bowled the silver sphere back up the path, towards the other two Yeti. He stood perfectly still.

The three Yetis lumbered closer and closer. Almost brushing against him, they lumbered up the path, after the sphere. The Doctor heaved a sigh of relief. 'It worked!' he said to himself in mild astonishment. Then he ran off down the path after Jamie.

Khrisong hurried across the courtyard to the main doors where Rapalchan, one of his young warriors, was keeping guard.

'Rapalchan! Has the Doctor returned?' he asked impatiently.

The sentry shook his head. 'No, Khrisong. No one has entered or left!'

Khrisong paused, indecisively. A man of action above all, he felt baffled and frustrated. Terrible perils menaced his beloved Monastery, and he could do nothing to fight them. Instead he was forced to rely on the promises of this strange Doctor, a madman springing from nowhere. Even the trusty Thomni had turned against him, led astray by that devil-girl Victoria.

Glaring round the courtyard he found a new target

for his anger. The two old lamas, Sapan and Rinchen, were strolling placidly across the courtyard on their way to morning prayer. Nothing must disturb their invariable routine, thought Khrisong, even though the whole Monastery was in peril. He crossed over to them and asked, 'Where is the Abbot Songtsen?'

'We have not seen him for many long hours,' said Sapan.

'Indeed, that is so,' agreed Rinchen. 'No doubt he seeks guidance from the Master Padmasambvha.'

Khrisong laughed scornfully. 'Seeks guidance – or seeks to evade his responsibilities?'

Sapan was shocked. 'You ought not to speak so,' he reproved.

'Why not? Has anyone ever seen this legendary immortal?' Khrisong walked quickly away, leaving the two old lamas staring after him aghast. What blasphemy! To query the very existence of the most holy one... Whatever was the world coming to? Shaking their heads, the two old men went on inside the Monastery.

For a moment all was peaceful in the courtyard. It was the hour of morning prayer, and all those not on duty would be in the Great Hall. The silence was broken by a gentle tapping at the main door. A quiet voice said, 'Open. It is I, your Abbot Songtsen.' The astonished Rapalchan opened the door – it was indeed the Abbot. Songtsen entered. Songtsen brushed his hand lightly over the young sentry's face. 'You have not seen me, Rapalchan. None has entered, none has left.'

Rapalchan stood in a trance, eyes staring ahead, while Songtsen crossed the courtyard and entered the Monastery. Once he was out of sight, Rapalchan came to, with a little start and resumed his vigil. None had entered, none had left.

Minutes later, Songtsen stood at the side of the shrouded figure of Padmasambvha. 'You have done well, Songtsen,' the incredibly old voice whispered. 'The Great Intelligence takes on material form. Now it will grow and grow. For their own safety, our brothers must leave the Monastery.'

'I understand, Master,' said the Abbot tonelessly. 'And the strangers?'

'I will tell you how to deal with them *if* they return.'

Victoria paced impatiently up and down the cell. Angrily she turned to Thomni who sat placidly on the floor in the posture of meditation.

'How can you take everything so quietly?' she demanded. 'After the way Khrisong spoke to you...'

'Khrisong carries many burdens,' said Thomni gently. 'Their weight makes him angry. He knows in his heart we are innocent. When his anger cools, he will release us.'

'Oh, will he? Well, if you think I'm sitting here quietly until he has a change of heart...'

Thomni looked at her in mild surprise. 'There is nothing else we can do, Miss Victoria. What is written is written...' He returned to his meditation.

There was a rattle at the door. Victoria looked up alertly. If they gave her the slightest chance… Rinchen entered, with a tray of food and drink. Eagerly Victoria seized one of the stone beakers. 'Oh, good, I'm so thirsty.' She drained the beaker at a gulp.

For a moment she stood gasping, her hand at her throat. 'The taste,' she gasped. 'So strange…' Suddenly she crumpled to the floor.

Horrified, Thomni knelt beside her. 'Miss Victoria, Miss Victoria…' She was quite still. Rinchen hovered indecisively. 'I will fetch help. Stay with her, Thomni.' The old lama scuttled off, leaving the door open behind him in his panic. Thomni went to the bed to fetch a blanket. He heard movement behind him and turned. Victoria was on her feet and by the door, her eyes sparkling with mischief. 'Sorry, Thomni,' she said, and nipped through the door, slamming and barring it behind her.

In the Great Hall, all the warrior monks and lamas were assembled, summoned by the Abbot Songtsen.

'I have sought guidance from the Master Padmasambvha,' he was saying solemnly. 'In his wisdom he has told me that there is no defence against the Yeti. We must flee at once, or we will all be slain.'

'No!' There was a shout from the doorway and they turned to see Khrisong. 'The Doctor has returned. He brings with him a way to fight this evil.'

The Abbot said sternly, 'Khrisong, the Master has decided…'

'The Master, always the Master,' interrupted Khrisong. 'I have felt the strength of these Yeti. See, I bear their scars on my arm. Yet I will not meekly turn away. I mean to fight! Who is with me? Come!'

A confused babble broke out in the Hall. But only a few of the warrior monks followed Khrisong as he strode out. The rest, afraid to defy their Abbot, stayed with the lamas and Songtsen.

The Abbot's voice cut through the noise. 'Brothers, Khrisong has been led astray by the strangers. He has forgotten his vows of obedience. Follow him, and bring him back to the path of wisdom! I will pray for guidance.' In a confused mass, monks and lamas poured excitedly from the Great Hall. Songtsen was left standing alone.

At once he closed his eyes, and went into a state of trance.

'Advise me, Padmasambvha,' he implored. 'Khrisong turns his warriors from the path of obedience. Not all of them will obey your command to go…'

From all around him, he heard the ghostly voice of Padmasambvha. 'If they will not be led from the Monastery – then they must be driven. This is what you must do…'

The Doctor and Jamie were waiting in the courtyard amidst a scene of utter confusion. A little crowd of monks and lamas milled about arguing and disputing. Some supported the Abbot, some were for following Khrisong.

The Doctor looked round in amazement. 'What's going on?' he said wonderingly.

'Search me,' said Jamie. 'Seems they've all gone daft.' Khrisong shouldered his way through the throng, a little knot of warriors around him. 'We must act quickly, Doctor. The Abbot has ordered us to evacuate the Monastery…'

He was interrupted by a frantic knocking and scrabbling at the doors. A faint voice called, 'Let me in. Please, let me in!'

Cautiously Khrisong opened the doors. A tattered, scarecrow figure staggered inside, and collapsed at their feet. It was Travers.

The Doctor and Jamie bent over him. He was in a terrible state, ragged, dirty and bleeding. He had tumbled down the mountain like a falling boulder, with no concern for his own safety. His lips were cracked, his eyes wide and staring, filled with the recollection of that horrible living mass that was bubbling and growing in the cave…

'Pyramid,' he muttered feverishly. 'It was growing… growing… the noise…' Travers' head lolled back, and he fainted dead away.

Jamie was thoroughly confused. 'What was all that about, Doctor?'

Before the Doctor could reply, there came a further shock. The Abbot Songtsen appeared. 'Seize the strangers,' he ordered. 'They must all be locked up at once. The girl Victoria has escaped. She too must be taken and imprisoned.'

At once utter pandemonium broke out. Everyone started talking and shouting at once.

'Victoria escaped?' yelled Jamie furiously. 'Escaped from where? Where is she? What's been going on?'

'Abbot Songtsen, please,' called the Doctor. 'You really must listen to me.' The Doctor's voice was drowned in the general babble. Khrisong shouldered him aside, and forced his way through the little crowd to the Abbot.

'I cannot allow this!' he protested fiercely.

The Abbot's voice was stern. '*You* cannot allow? These are the orders of the Master. You *must* obey.'

'These people can help us, Lord Abbot.'

'The Master says there is *no* help against the Yeti. He orders us to leave or we will all die.'

A frightened murmuring from the monks and lamas showed the effect of his words. Songtsen saw that he had the upper hand. 'Take the strangers and lock them up,' he ordered.

A horde of panic-stricken monks descended upon the Doctor and Jamie, and bustled them away, ignoring their protests and those of Khrisong. The Doctor was almost carried off towards the cell, and Jamie, struggling furiously, was bundled along after him. Other monks picked up the unconscious Travers and carried him along, too.

The Abbot turned to Khrisong and the little group of rebellious warriors around him. 'Khrisong! Defy me no further. Take your warriors and find the girl.' For a moment it seemed that Khrisong would still refuse. Then, defeated, he bowed his head, and led his warriors away.

Except for the sentry at the doors, the Abbot was now alone in the great courtyard. He walked across to the doors and said to the sentry, 'Go and join in the search, my son.' He passed his hand lightly over the sentry's face, and the young monk froze for a moment, then ran off after his fellows. Once he was out of sight, Songtsen unbarred the great doors and then opened them wide. The Monastery of Det-sen was defenceless. 'It is done, Master,' said the Abbot Songtsen. Then he walked slowly away.

Since her escape from the cell, Victoria had been hiding in the empty guest quarters, uncertain what to do with herself once she was free. She wondered where everyone was, not realising that Travers, the Doctor and Jamie had just returned to the Monastery.

Eventually, she crept cautiously out into the corridor and moved towards the courtyard. Soon she began to hear the noise and shouting of the excited monks. Afraid to venture further, she waited. Suddenly the noise started coming nearer. She could hear yells and shouts. 'Find her. Find the devil girl!' With a shock, Victoria realised that they were hunting *her*. Terrified, she turned and fled, the sounds of pursuit echoing behind her.

For what seemed an endless time she was hunted up and down the gloomy corridors. More than once she eluded her pursuers by hiding in some dark corner, while they all raced by. But they always seemed to pick up her trail again.

By the time she managed to shake them off, Victoria was in a part of the Monastery that she had never visited before. She found herself in a little windowless room, lit only by flickering prayer lamps. On the walls were rich hangings and tapestries. All around were carved statues, devil masks, rare ornaments. Victoria knew enough about antiques to realise that the contents of the little room were virtually priceless.

At the far end of the room, she saw a pair of ornately carved double doors, Victoria looked at them curiously, wondering what was beyond them. She decided not to try and find out. This place was quiet enough, but it was far too spooky to be comfortable. She turned to leave, and found that she couldn't move. Something, some force, held her unmoving.

'Enter, my child,' said a voice. It came from nowhere and yet from everywhere. It was quiet and gentle, yet it filled the room. The doors opened before her of their own accord. 'Come in,' said the voice again. 'You *must* come in, you have no alternative.'

Victoria tried to hang back, but the invisible force made her walk slowly into the Inner Sanctum. Ahead of her she could see the raised dais, the golden throne with its seated figure. She was drawn closer and closer. The canopy round the throne had been pulled back. The seated figure raised its head and looked at her. Victoria was the first in many hundred years to look upon the face of Padmasambvha. She opened her mouth in a gasp of pure terror, too frightened even to scream…

9

Attack of the Yeti

Victoria's first thought was that the man before her was incredibly old. Older than Sapan or Rinchen, or any of the other venerable old men at the Monastery. Older than anyone she had ever seen or imagined. So old that the shrunken body seemed like that of a child, swaddled inside the long, flowing robes.

The face was quite incredible. Completely hairless, with huge forehead, sunken cheeks and bony jaw. In contrast to the wizened face and shrunken body, the eyes were huge and dark and alive, shining with the blaze of an almost superhuman intelligence. The Master Padmasambvha had indeed gone beyond the flesh. His body was merely the worn-out husk which barely contained his soul and spirit.

He looked up at Victoria, and smiled with a curious gentleness. 'Do not be afraid, my child. Why do you come here?'

Victoria tried to babble some explanation. 'I'm sorry, I was lost, and I was afraid. They were chasing me, you see, and…'

Gently, Padmasambvha interrupted her. 'You need help, do you not?'

'Yes, I'm afraid I do,' said Victoria thankfully. 'You see, I can't find the Doctor and…'

Padmasambvha held up his hand, cutting her off. 'One moment, child.'

He leaned forward, brooding over the board in front of him. 'The courtyard is empty, and the gates are open,' he said mysteriously. Victoria leaned forward, peering at the model landscape with its tiny figures.

'I must do what I am compelled to do,' said Padmasambvha sadly. He picked up one of the little figures from the board.

'What is it?' asked Victoria curiously. She was getting over her fear now.

There was something pathetic about the old man. Yet, at the same time, something frightening, and unpredictable too.

'Come and see,' invited the Master, holding up the little figure.

Victoria came closer and looked at it. 'It's one of those horrible creatures – a Yeti.'

Again Padmasambvha gave that curiously sad smile. 'That is so, my child. But you have not seen it.' He passed his hand gently in front of her eyes. Immediately Victoria went into a trance, her eyes wide open and staring. Padmasambvha placed the Yeti model down in the courtyard of the miniature Monastery.

He reached out for another model. 'I must do what I am compelled to do,' whispered Padmasambvha again.

*

The courtyard of the Monastery still stood empty. The doors were open wide. One after another, four of the Yeti lumbered into the courtyard. Once inside, they split up, each making for a different part of the Monastery, as if by some prearranged plan.

Things were uncomfortably crowded in the little cell. Travers lay on the bed. He had fallen into a deep, exhausted sleep, broken by occasional muttering and twitching.

The Doctor perched on the wooden stool by the bed, watching Travers thoughtfully. Thomni sat cross-legged by the wall in his meditation position. Jamie was pacing up and down the cell, pausing now and again to bang on the door, or yell through the grille.

'So that's why they locked up poor Victoria,' he was saying to Thomni. 'She was telling the truth, you know. Those wee balls *can* make you put them back in the Yeti. One of them nearly did it to me, didn't it, Doctor?'

The Doctor nodded absently, his eyes still fixed on the face of the sleeper.

Suddenly Travers opened his eyes, and stared in amazement at the Doctor. 'Where am I? What happened to me?'

'We were rather hoping you could tell us that,' said the Doctor gently.

Travers shook his head vaguely. 'I left the Monastery then... it's no use... it's all a blank... there's just a feeling of evil... I felt a shadow on my mind. I felt as if I might drown…'

'Aye, man, but what did you see?' asked Jamie impatiently. 'Where did all this happen?'

Travers closed his eyes again. 'I don't know… I can't… I'm so tired…' His eyes closed and sank back into sleep.

'What do you think?' asked Jamie.

The Doctor sighed, and scratched his head. 'He must have seen something very nasty indeed, I fear. Perhaps whatever's behind all this trouble we're having. If only he could tell us.'

There came a tremendous crash from somewhere inside the Monastery. It was followed by shouts of alarm, cries of fear, and the sound of running feet. 'The Yeti are coming,' yelled a panic-stricken voice. 'Flee, my brothers, flee!'

Jamie rattled at the door. 'What's going on? Let us out of here.'

But the Doctor, with a pleased expression, had pulled his detection device from under the bed and was carefully noting the readings.

Khrisong's face appeared briefly at the grille. 'The Yeti have broken into the Monastery. Stay where you are, you are safe there.'

'What about Victoria,' yelled Jamie frantically. 'Where is she? Have you found her?' But Khrisong had gone. Jamie turned back to the Doctor. 'Isn't there something we can…'

The Doctor hushed him with an upheld hand. Jamie saw that he was bent intently over the detection device, studying every little flicker of the dials.

The Abbot Songtsen, Khrisong and most of the monks and lamas, were gathered together in the Great Hall. From throughout the Monastery came the sound of destruction, as the Yeti carried on their rampage. Occasionally there was a scream, as some unfortunate monk was caught in their path. Khrisong tried to organise his warriors into a defensive force, but they were all too panic-stricken.

He said bitterly to Songtsen, 'Forgive me, my Abbot. I have failed you.'

The Abbot looked at him pityingly. 'You have not failed, my son. This disaster was written. Man cannot alter his destiny.'

Meanwhile, the Yeti raged unhindered through the Monastery. Dormitories were wrecked, statues cast down, priceless treasures mutilated and destroyed. Yet they did not seem intent on taking life. They attacked only those who attacked them, or sought to hinder their work of methodical destruction. It was in the storage cellars that most terrible havoc was wreaked. The Yeti smashed open food barrels, burst water tanks so that the food cellars were flooded, and mixed fuel, food, clothing and medicines into one unusable pile.

Then, as if their work were done, they began to withdraw from the Monastery.

A terrified monk rushed into the Great Hall to give the news to the Abbot. 'The Yeti are falling back,' he cried.

'Come, brethren, do not be afraid,' said the Abbot. He led his little band from the Great Hall into the courtyard.

All but two of the Yeti were gone. These two stood waiting by a great golden statue of Buddha that dominated the courtyard, the Buddha that was the very spirit and symbol of Det-sen Monastery. The appearance of the Abbot and his followers seemed to serve as a signal. The remaining two Yeti lumbered forward, seized the statue in their mighty paws, and began to tilt it forward. The old lama, Rinchen, ran forward from the crowd in horror. 'No! No!' he cried. 'You shall not.' Stretching out his feeble hands, he made a vain attempt to prevent the great golden figure from falling. Slowly the Buddha crashed to the stones of the courtyard, crushing the life from old Rinchen in the process. The head of the Buddha was smashed from the body. It rolled slowly across the courtyard. The two Yeti turned and left.

Khrisong looked from the broken statue to the broken body of Rinchen. 'The Monastery of Det-sen is accursed,' he said bitterly. 'It is time for us to leave.'

Padmasambvha was communing with the Great Intelligence. Beside him stood Victoria, unseeing and unhearing in her trance.

'Now it is complete,' whispered Padmasambvha. 'Now the monks will leave. By nightfall the Monastery will be deserted, the entire mountain yours.' He turned his attention to Victoria. 'And what of you and your friends, my poor child? The Doctor is not so easily frightened as my poor monks. Therefore you must help me. Together we will make sure that he leaves. Come closer.'

Unable to resist, Victoria stepped forward.

Jamie watched impatiently as Thomni finished scratching a plan of the Monastery on the cell wall with a piece of chalk fished from the Doctor's capacious pocket.

'This is the courtyard,' said Thomni, pointing. 'We are here – to the south. The north lies – here.' And he chalked an 'N' on the map.

The Doctor took the chalk from him and drew a line across the map.

'Does your science provide an answer, Doctor?' asked Thomni.

'Only half an answer, I'm afraid. We know that the transmissions come from *somewhere* on this line. But we need a second reading, a cross reference to give us the actual place. That could give us the *where*.' Absentmindedly, the Doctor scratched his head with the piece of chalk. 'Of course we still won't have the most important thing.'

'Oh aye, and what's that?' said Jamie impatiently.

The Doctor looked at him in surprise. 'The *why* of course. That's what we really need to know.'

Travers came to life with a sudden start. He sat up, looked round, and said cheerily, 'Hullo, Doctor, Jamie. How are you all?'

'Oh, fine, just fine,' said Jamie dryly.

'What's going on?' said Travers. 'What are we doing here?'

'There's been a spot of trouble,' said the Doctor gently.

'With the Yeti,' added Jamie,

'Oh, really,' said Travers. 'Must have missed it all while I was sleeping.'

'You had a spot of trouble yourself,' prompted the Doctor. 'On the mountainside. You saw something pretty nasty. Do you remember?'

'Not a thing,' said Travers. 'Got a bit of a headache, actually. Think I'll get a breath of fresh air.' He got up, went to the door and tried to open it. 'I say,' he said indignantly, 'do you chaps realise we're locked in?'

In the courtyard, the monks had managed to move the heavy statue. Some of them were lifting Rinchen's body on to a stretcher. Khrisong's head was bowed in grief.

'Do not blame yourself,' said the Abbot Songtsen. 'Death is inevitable.' He turned to the monks with the stretcher. 'Rinchen will accompany us on our journey. There will be time to mourn our brother. The rest of you gather what is needed. Save what provisions you can. Soon it will be the hour for meditation. Then we must depart.'

'What of the strangers?' asked Sapan.

'They will be taken with us to a place of safety.'

'And the Master Padmasambvha?'

'His powers are great,' said the Abbot. 'He will

remain.'

There was a sudden stir amongst the crowd. Many of the monks fell to their knees. Turning, Songtsen saw that Victoria had come into the courtyard. In her hands was the holy ghanta. A murmur of awe swept through the crowd.

For a moment Victoria stood immobile, eyes wide and staring hands outstretched. Then she spoke. But the voice that came from her lips was that of Padmasambvha. 'I have chosen to speak to you through the lips of this maiden,' said the low, compelling voice that seemed to come from all around them. 'She holds the holy ghanta. Bear it away with you for safe keeping. Treat her with kindness – she and the other strangers are innocent of malice. They wish to help you against the Yeti but I tell you there is no help. Det-sen must be abandoned. When the wind destroys its nest, the bird will build another.'

Victoria fell silent. She tottered, and the monks rushed to support her.

'Release the strangers,' said Songtsen. 'Bid them make ready to depart.'

Victoria was in the guest room, sitting on the bed and gazing straight in front of her, when the Doctor, Jamie and Travers were brought in by Khrisong and Thomni.

'Victoria, are you all right?' asked Jamie anxiously. She did not move,

'Victoria,' said the Doctor. The sound of *his* voice provoked an instant reaction.

'Doctor,' she said, 'there is great danger. You must take me away! Take me away!' She spoke in a sort of formal chant. She stopped, and fell into her silent trance. 'Victoria, what is it? What's the matter?' said Jamie. She ignored him.

'Khrisong, how long has she been like this?' asked the Doctor.

But before Khrisong could reply, Victoria reacted once more to the Doctor's voice.

'Doctor, there is great danger. Take me away from here. Take me away.' Like a switched-off record she fell silent.

'She's reacting to my voice,' said the Doctor. He moved away. 'I'd better start whispering.'

'She is still in a trance,' said Khrisong gravely. Briefly he told the Doctor what had happened.

'She must have reached the Sanctum,' said Thomni. 'She has seen the Holy Padmasambvha.'

The Doctor looked up sharply. 'Padmasambvha, the Master? Surely he must have died long ago – I met him on my last visit, and he was incredibly old then. He can't have lived for another three hundred years.'

'Padmasambvha is ageless, Doctor,' said Khrisong gravely. 'But how could you have known him three hundred years ago? Are you ageless, too?'

The Doctor didn't reply. 'Padmasambvha – still here,' he muttered to himself. 'Why does nobody *tell* me anything?' He moved to the door. 'Take care of Victoria for me, Jamie,' he whispered. 'I shan't be long.'

'Can you no' help her?' demanded Jamie.

'I think so, Jamie. But I have to find out something first. Khrisong, will you walk with me for a moment?'

As they walked along the corridor together, the Doctor said, 'Khrisong, a while ago you wanted my help. Now, you're preparing to leave. Don't you want to save the Monastery any more?'

'I must obey the Abbot,' said Khrisong. 'He wishes us to leave.'

'Somebody wishes it,' replied the Doctor. 'That's why all this was arranged. To get you to leave. That's why someone opened the gates to the Yeti, so they could spoil all your supplies and terrify your monks. Are you going to do what this someone wants?'

Khrisong was silent.

'I am very close to success,' said the Doctor. 'But I still need help.'

They stopped at a junction of corridors. 'If you need my help, you shall have it,' said Khrisong.

The Doctor smiled. 'Thank you. Now if you'll excuse me – I must visit an old friend; one I haven't seen for many years.'

'You go to the Sanctum, Doctor? Do you wish me to accompany you?'

'That won't be necessary, Khrisong. I already know the way.' With a farewell nod, the Doctor set off.

As he walked through the wrecked and deserted Monastery his mind was a ferment of ideas. Padmasambvha, still alive! He must be nearly four hundred years old – an incredible feat, even for a Tibetan master. Padmasambvha was a good man, thought the Doctor. One of the best men I've ever known. Who or what could change him? Lost in thought, the Doctor walked on towards the Inner Sanctum.

In the Sanctum itself, the frail body of Padmasambvha was twisting and writhing on his chair, locked in some terrible inner struggle. 'Oh, Great Intelligence,' he gasped, 'you promised me release, yet still you hold your grip on my old body. Is not your plan complete? Will not the mountain content you…'

A vision of the cave on the mountain filled the Master's mind. The glutinous living mass still seeped from the pyramid. More and more and more… it filled the cave… it was filling the tunnel. When would it stop? How much territory would it cover? 'You said *only* the Mountain for your Experiment,' shrieked Padmasambvha. 'If you do not stop, you will cover the planet. You have lied to me… tricked me.' The sound of hellish cosmic laughter seemed to fill his ears. The old Master slumped in his chair. In an appalled whisper, he said, 'I have brought the world to its end!'

For some time he sat on the golden throne, his breath only a shallow flutter. Then his mind sensed someone in the Anteroom. He looked at the doors. 'Enter,' he whispered, and the doors opened.

The Doctor walked slowly towards the throne. He looked at the shrunken figure upon it, saddened by the toll the years had taken of his old friend. Padmasambvha had been old when the Doctor first met him – well over a hundred. But he had still been vigorous, clear-skinned and bright-eyed. Now he was a shattered husk of a man, his life prolonged beyond any natural length. But why, the Doctor wondered, and how?

Padmasambvha's voice was a little more than a breath. 'Greetings, Doctor. It is good to see your face after so long.'

The Doctor said quietly, 'What has happened to you, old friend?'

Padmasambvha could speak only with a tremendous effort. 'I have been kept alive,' he whispered feebly. 'I did not know... did not realise... Intelligence... formless... on the Astral plane... it wished for form... substance... said it was experiment... long life and knowledge, in return for my help.'

The Doctor leaned forward. The thin reedy voice was scarcely audible. It was as though something was trying to stop the Master from speaking. The thin whisper went on...'Refused to let me go... on and on... not experiment but conquest!' The last word came out in a sudden gasp.

Then the body of Padmasambvha writhed and twisted. It actually rose in the air and hung suspended. Then it dropped to the chair, limp, like a rag doll.

The Doctor leaned forward urgently. He felt the heart, the pulse, held his magnifying glass before the withered lips to test for breath. Nothing. Grim-faced, the Doctor turned and left the room.

For a moment there was silence. Then suddenly the body of Padmasambvha jerked and twisted. It sat bolt upright on the throne filled with new vigour. The eyes that glared after the Doctor were ablaze with malevolence. The Great Intelligence was back in control.

10

Peril on the Mountain

Jamie sat uneasily watching the still-motionless Victoria. They were alone. Travers had wandered off somewhere. Jamie had tried speaking to her loudly and commandingly, gently and persuasively, all to no avail. In sudden exasperation, he picked up a stool and slammed it down on the ground just behind her. The stool shattered to pieces. Victoria didn't stir.

'What on earth are you doing, Jamie?' He looked up to see the Doctor in the doorway. Before Jamie could answer, Victoria reacted to the Doctor's voice. 'Doctor, there is great danger! You must take me away! You must take me away! Take me away!' This time there was an added note of sheer hysteria in her voice.

'You've got to do something, Doctor,' said Jamie desperately. 'I've tried everything and she takes no notice at all. She sounds as if she's getting worse!'

The Doctor went over to the bed, and stood over Victoria. He said gently, 'Victoria, my dear—'

This time her voice was a scream of terror. 'Doctor – take me away! Take me away!'

'No, Victoria!' There was a whiplash crack of authority in the Doctor's voice. Victoria stopped her screaming, and gazed up at him in panic… 'Listen to me, Victoria,' said the Doctor firmly. 'You are no longer in the Monastery, you are back in the TARDIS. You are safe, do you understand. Safe in the TARDIS.'

She looked up at him wonderingly. 'Safe?' she whispered.

'Look at me,' murmured the Doctor soothingly. 'You are tired, your eyes are closing, let yourself relax…'

Victoria's eyes closed and her head nodded. So did Jamie's. The Doctor jabbed him in the ribs. 'Not you, Jamie!'

Jamie came awake with a jerk, grinned sheepishly, and said, 'What now?'

'I've got to try to erase this implanted fear, if I can,' said the Doctor. 'It's increasing all the time.'

'Suppose you can't?' Jamie asked anxiously.

'We'll have to do as she says and take her away. Otherwise she'll go out of her mind.'

Jamie looked at him in horror. 'That's the object of all this,' said the Doctor gently. 'To make sure we leave with the others.'

He snapped his fingers in front of Victoria's face. Her eyes opened. 'Listen, Victoria, you are not in the TARDIS. You are in the cell with Thomni. Do you understand?' Victoria nodded slowly. The Doctor went on in the same compelling tone. 'Jamie and I have come to release you. We have taken you back to the guest room. You have been dozing. You will wake up in a moment, happy but still a little tired. Do you understand?' Again Victoria nodded. She slipped back slowly on to the bed, her eyes closing. She was asleep.

'I've erased the memory of whatever happened after she left the cell,' said the Doctor. 'She should be all right now.'

Jamie looked at him with respect. 'I didna realise you could do that sort of thing, Doctor.'

'I don't *like* to do it, Jamie. It's a serious thing to tamper with the mind. But in an emergency like this…'

Suddenly Victoria sat up, yawning. She smiled at them. 'I must have dropped off. I am glad you came and got me out of that cell. I was so bored…'

She turned to Jamie who was staring at her open-mouthed. 'What are you gawping at, Jamie? Anyone would think there was something wrong with me!'

The Doctor chuckled. 'Stay with her, Jamie. I've got work to do.' Gathering up his detection device, he slipped away before Jamie could ask him what he'd discovered.

The Doctor found Travers on one of the observation platforms, gazing up the mountainside with his old binoculars. 'They're still up there, Doctor,' he said. 'Look.' He handed over the field glasses.

Peering through them, the Doctor could see several Yeti dotted about the mountainside, motionless and waiting… 'I must go back up there,' he said softly. 'One more reading and I can track their control source. I could do with some help.'

Travers looked at him uneasily. 'What about the

boy?'

'He's staying here to look after Victoria. They'll leave with the monks.'

Travers nodded. 'All right, Doctor, I'm your man. I reckon I owe you something.'

Some time later, the Doctor and Travers were well on the way up the mountainside. They rounded a bend and saw three Yeti guarding the path a little way ahead. The Doctor turned to Travers. 'Now we need to provoke it enough to send out a signal. If you'll take the reading…' He started to hand over the black box.

Travers shook his head. 'I don't know how that thing works, Doctor. You take the readings and I'll stir 'em up.'

The Doctor looked dubious. 'I don't like to ask you to take the risk…'

'Rot,' said Travers stoutly, 'I can take care of myself.'

He came out from behind the boulders and marched boldly up to one of the Yeti. It didn't move. 'Boo!' Travers yelled. Still nothing. Then, suddenly, all the Yeti came to life. They started moving forwards. 'Are you getting your readings, Doctor?' yelled Travers, backing away in alarm. He jumped aside, out of their way.

The Doctor, head bent over the flickering dials, did not reply. He seemed oblivious of the little group of Yeti marching straight towards him. 'Look out, Doctor,' Travers yelled. The Yeti marched on, past the Doctor, ignoring him completely. They veered off at a tangent across the mountainside, and disappeared from sight behind some boulders. Travers shook his head. 'Wonder what caused *that*?' he muttered. He went back to the Doctor, who was still studying his dials. 'I said did you get your reading?' he asked. The Doctor nodded, his face worried.

'Yes,' he said, 'I'm afraid I did. We'd better be getting back.'

Followed by a puzzled Travers, the Doctor started scrambling down the path. He was frowning furiously, lost in some very unpleasant thoughts.

Supervised by the Abbot Songtsen, a sad little procession of monks and warriors was assembling in the courtyard. They were bundled up in their warmest robes. The young warriors were making up heavy packs, containing such provisions as they had been able to salvage from the wreckage. Jamie and Victoria stood looking on.

Khrisong entered the courtyard from the Monastery and hurried over to them. 'My warriors have searched every room. There is no sign of the Doctor, or of Travers,' he whispered. Going over to Songtsen he said, 'It is as you wished, my Abbot. Every room in the Monastery is empty.'

'It is well,' said Songtsen gravely. 'I will ask a final blessing of the Master, Padmasambvha, then we shall leave.' He went inside the Monastery.

Victoria frowned. 'Master? Padmasambvha? That sounds...'

'Dinna think about it,' said Jamie fiercely. 'Think

about something else. Anything!'

Victoria looked at him in puzzlement. Luckily there was an immediate distraction. The Doctor and Travers came into the courtyard. Victoria rushed up to the Doctor and hugged him in delight. 'You're back! Where have you been?'

The Doctor disengaged himself with an absent-minded 'There, there,' and went over to Khrisong and Thomni. 'I've found it,' he said urgently. 'Khrisong, I've found the source of the transmissions controlling the Yeti!'

Khrisong indicated the little procession forming up for departure. 'I fear you are too late.'

'You don't understand,' interrupted the Doctor. 'As I suspected all along, it's here, in the Monastery.' He looked at his box. 'It's transmitting now, at this very moment.'

Khrisong looked round. 'But we are all here, in this courtyard… all but… the Abbot Songtsen!'

The Doctor nodded. 'I fear so. Now that the Master is dead, he's the only one left.'

'The Master dead?' said Thomni.

The Doctor nodded sadly. 'I should have told you earlier. We'd better find Songtsen.'

'No!' said Khrisong fiercely. 'I will deal with him. It is my right.'

The Doctor looked at him dubiously. 'He too has great powers,' he said.

'He is still my Abbot,' said Khrisong confidently. 'He will not harm me.' He turned and left. The Doctor was worried. Could Khrisong deal with the Abbot? The Doctor knew that if Padmasambvha had been alive, Khrisong wouldn't have stood a chance. But since it was only Songtsen...

Travers said suddenly, 'Songtsen! He was *with* them He was with the Yeti on the mountainside. And there was a cave...'

A look of horror came over Travers' face as memory flooded back to him. Briefly, he described seeing Songtsen escorted by Yeti, and the growing, swelling horror in the cave.

'If Songtsen can control the Yeti, he's more dangerous than I'd thought,' said the Doctor. 'I think I'd better go and help Khrisong.'

Khrisong marched into the Anteroom, a burly, warlike figure, sword in hand. He towered over the frail figure of the Abbot who stood, in an attitude of prayer, before the doors to the Sanctum. 'You must come with me, Lord Abbot,' said Khrisong, gruffly. 'You must come away from this place.'

Songtsen looked up at him with mild surprise. 'What madness is this?'

'The Doctor has discovered your guilt,' said Khrisong. 'You must answer to the brethren for your crimes.'

He seized the Abbot as if to drag him away by force. Then a voice spoke out of the air. 'Khrisong!'

Khrisong glared round. 'Padmasambvha. The Doctor told us you were dead.'

'I am deathless, Khrisong.' There was a cold gloating note in the voice.

'Do not try to frighten me. I demand to know what is happening here!'

Songtsen was appalled. 'Demand, Khrisong? You are in the presence of the Master.'

'A Master of the Yeti?' demanded Khrisong. 'A Master who has destroyed his own monastery?'

Songtsen turned towards the closed door. 'Forgive him, oh Master.'

'Of course,' said the cold voice. 'But our brother must not depart thinking that I am other than I am. Bring him to me, Songtsen!'

Songtsen said tonelessly, 'I obey, master.' Looking down at him, Khrisong saw that the Abbot seemed almost in a state of trance, his eyes staring sightlessly ahead.

'What is this?' he growled suspiciously.

The doors to the Sanctum swung open. 'You may enter,' said Songtsen. 'But give me your sword. You may not go armed into the presence of Padmasambvha.'

Khrisong hesitated. 'Do you fear us, Khrisong?' asked the voice. 'We are two old men!'

Khrisong handed over his sword. He went towards the doors. Songtsen, the sword in his hands, was behind him.

Khrisong stopped cautiously on the threshold to the Sanctum. He peered through the gloom at the figure on the throne. His eyes widened in awe. 'Padmasambvha,' he whispered. 'So you are not dead!'

'No, my son, but you are,' said the cold voice.

Behind Khrisong, Songtsen raised the sword, and thrust with savage force. Khrisong gasped and wheeled round. His eyes, filled with pain and unbelief, fixed on those of his Abbot. Khrisong took a couple of tottering steps forward and collapsed. The doors to the Sanctum swung to.

In the Sanctum, the body of Padmasambvha writhed on the throne. For a moment a different voice emerged from the withered lips, as the personality of the real Padmasambvha broke through. 'Why do you make me do this? Release me, I beg of you...'

Then, as the Intelligence reasserted its control, the cold voice filled the room. 'You have done well, Songtsen. Take the monks from the Monastery, and never return.'

In the Anteroom, Songtsen said, 'I obey, master.' He was about to leave when the Doctor, Thomni and Jamie rushed into the room. They found him standing over Khrisong's body, the bloodstained sword in his hands.

The little group stopped at the threshold, appalled. 'Lord Abbot!' called Thomni in horror. He rushed to kneel by Khrisong's body. Songtsen looked down in horror. 'What has happened? Who has slain Khrisong?' he asked.

Thomni looked up. 'You killed him, you!' he sobbed.

Songtsen looked in utter amazement at the bloody sword in his hands... 'I?' he said wonderingly.

A cold voice filled the room. 'Slay them, Songtsen.

Slay them all!'

The blankness of trance came over Songtsen's face and he raised the sword. 'Kill! Kill! Kill!' he hissed.

'Look out!' yelled the Doctor. He dodged the blow and grabbed the Abbot's sword arm.

Despite his modest size, the Doctor could exert amazing strength when he needed to. But he was helpless in Songtsen's grip. The frail old body was vibrating with supernatural force. Thomni and Jamie, both young and strong, joined in the struggle. It took every ounce of their combined strengths to subdue the Abbot and wrench the sword from his hands. Suddenly Songtsen slumped in their grip. The Doctor stood back panting. 'Get him out of here,' he gasped. 'Quickly!'

Jamie and Thomni dragged the Abbot away. The Doctor looked grimly at the closed doors to the Sanctum. 'I was wrong, then,' he thought grimly. 'Whatever is controlling Padmasambvha will not let him die!'

The Doctor turned and left, and the Anteroom was filled with the mad, icy laughter of the Intelligence.

As the Doctor walked along the corridor he met an excited Travers. 'You'd better come at once, Doctor. There's going to be a riot!'

11

The Final Battle

A confused and angry crowd filled the courtyard. They surrounded Jamie and Thomni, and the frightened and confused Songtsen. 'Indeed, it is true, brothers,' Thomni was shouting. 'Khrisong *was* slain by the Abbot. But Songtsen was under an evil spell, placed on him by the Master.'

One of the young warrior monks thrust himself to the front of the crowd. 'Tell us it is not so, my Abbot,' he implored.

For a moment Songtsen gazed at him uncomprehendingly. Then, grabbing the still bloody sword from Thomni's hand he hissed, 'Kill! Kill! Kill!' and swung the sword at the astonished monk. Once again it took the combined efforts of several strong young warriors to hold down the frail body. Then the fit was over and the Abbot went limp.

A roar of fear and terror rose from the crowd. 'He is bewitched,' they shouted. 'He is possessed by demons. Slay him now before he kills us all.' Another warrior stepped forward, sword raised high above Songtsen's head. Ignoring the weapon, Jamie gave the man a hearty shove that sent him staggering back into the crowd.

'I'm thinking we've had enough killing,' he said grimly. 'Stand back!'

'Do not interfere, stranger,' said the monk angrily, and the warriors began to close in. Jamie slipped the highland dagger from his stocking, and shoved the Abbot behind him.

'Wait, my brothers,' called Thomni, but the warriors would not listen.

As the Doctor entered the courtyard with Travers, he took in the ugly situation at a glance. In times of crisis, his normally modest and unassuming personality took on a new force.

'Stop this nonsense at once,' he ordered, pushing through the crowd.

'Your Abbot is not responsible for his crime. Neither for that matter is the Master, Padmasambvha. Both are being controlled by a greater force.'

The monks fell silent. 'What must we do, Doctor?' asked old Sapan.

'Leave the Monastery. There is great evil here. One day soon, if I am successful, you will be able to return.'

'The Doctor is right, my brethren,' shouted Thomni. 'Let us obey him and leave now!'

There was a murmur of agreement. Their anger subsiding, the confused and frightened monks began to gather up their belongings. Thomni said, 'And what of you, Doctor?'

'I shall stay here,' said the Doctor simply. 'If this evil isn't stopped it will spread... And the root of it is here, in this Monastery.'

'Well, if you're staying, I'm staying too,' said Victoria firmly.

'Aye, and me!' added Jamie.

'I too will stay and help you, if I may, Doctor,' said Thomni.

The Doctor smiled. 'Thank you, all of you. It may be dangerous, but I won't pretend I'm not glad of your help.'

'What's the first step?' asked Jamie.

'There are things I need to know,' said the Doctor thoughtfully. 'And Songtsen is the only one who can tell me.'

'How will you make him do that, Doctor?' asked Thomni. 'His mind is controlled.'

The Doctor sighed. 'There's more than one kind of control, Thomni. Let's take him inside, shall we?'

Travers walked slowly back to his room. He was convinced that, for all his cleverness, the Doctor was wrong. The source of the evil wasn't some old monk in the Monastery, it was the evil throbbing mass in that cave up the mountain.

There was nothing Travers wanted less than to see that cave again. But he reckoned it was up to him. He picked up his rifle and loaded it. He'd blast that pyramid thing with a clip full of bullets, and see if that stopped it.

Unnoticed by the busy monks, Travers slipped out of the gate and began climbing up the mountain path. It was getting dark now. For a moment he stopped, and looked back longingly at the lights of the Monastery. Then, he began to climb the path, dreading what he might find at the end of his journey.

In the Great Hall, the Abbot Songtsen sat on a high-backed stone chair. His eyes were wide open and he stared unseeingly ahead of him. But this time, the voice he heard and obeyed came not from Padmasambvha, but from the Doctor.

'What about the robots, the false Yeti?' the Doctor was prompting.

'They were designed to serve the Intelligence. Their purpose was to frighten all travellers and pilgrims from Det-sen, lest they hinder the Great Plan.'

'And just what is this plan?' the Doctor asked.

'At first the Intelligence said that it wished only to create substance for itself – as an experiment. It wanted only the cave. Then it demanded the whole mountain. The Monastery, too. Its appetite is insatiable. It seeks to overwhelm the whole world.'

The Doctor remembered Travers' description of the glowing, ever-growing mass in the cave. He had a sudden horrific vision of the whole Earth, hanging in space, one heaving, pulsating mass. And what then? Suppose it travelled through space. All the planets in the Universe could be under threat. The Doctor shivered. Somehow he had to stop it.

'Tell me, Songtsen,' he said. 'How are the Yeti controlled?'

'By Padmasambvha.'

'What about the control units? Where did they come from?'

'Under the guidance of the Intelligence, the Master laboured for nearly three hundred years. He made the control units, the Yeti, all the other wonderful machines...'

'But there still has to be some kind of master transmitter,' insisted the Doctor. 'The power source that amplifies the commands of Padmasambvha's mind. Where is it?'

Songtsen said, 'It is in the Sanctum.'

The Doctor was puzzled. 'I've been in the Sanctum, very briefly, it's true, but I saw nothing.'

'There is a secret room...'

'Where is it, Songtsen? How do we get in there?'

There was no reply. The Abbot sat staring into space.

The Doctor leaned forward, his voice commanding. 'How do we reach the secret room, Songtsen? You must tell us. You *must* tell us...'

In the Inner Sanctum the body of Padmasambvha jerked into life as the Intelligence took over. The withered hand hovered over the board, picked up a Yeti and moved it down towards the Monastery.

Out on the mountain, in the fast-gathering dark, Travers plodded on, rifle in hand. Not that he really expected the weapon would do him any good against a Yeti. It was just that its presence gave him a certain comfort.

He heard the sound of huge shuffling feet ahead of him and dropped into cover. Two Yeti lumbered past, then another and another. Making for the Monastery, thought Travers. He hoped those poor devils of monks had got safely away. And what about that fellow, the Doctor? What were his plans?

Travers got to his feet and started to move on. As he climbed he became aware of something very strange. On the lower slopes of the mountain, it had been getting darker and darker as the night drew on. But now that he was actually getting closer to the cave it seemed to be getting lighter. It was as though the entire mountain was somehow glowing.

The strange light continued to increase. Then as he came within sight of the cave, Travers understood why. The cave itself was the source of the light.

The pulsating, glowing mass of the Intelligence's physical form was flooding out of the cave at an absolutely incredible rate. Spreading out from the cave, it seemed to be seeping into and absorbing the very substance of the mountain.

It was moving in both directions, upwards as if to consume the topmost peak of the mountain, and downwards too. If it went on spreading it would eventually ooze down the mountain slopes and engulf the entire Monastery.

Travers realised the foolishness of his plan to attack the pyramid in the cave. There was nothing he could do against the kind of power that was exultantly displayed here. Perhaps the Doctor had been right all along. Perhaps the Monastery did hold the key to it all. Travers remembered the Yeti he had seen trooping down the mountainside. With a sudden sense of urgency, he began to run back down the path.

In the Great Hall, the Doctor handed Songtsen over to the care of the old lama Sapan, who was now the leader of the monks. 'I have done my best to erase the memory of evil from his mind,' said the Doctor. 'But he will be troubled for a long time. He has suffered much.'

'We will care for him, Doctor,' promised Sapan. Two other lamas gently led the old Abbot out of the hall.

The Doctor turned to those left behind – Thomni, Jamie and Victoria. 'Now remember,' he said. 'As soon as *all* the monks and lamas are safely away, we'll have to make our attack on the control room of the Intelligence. You two lads have got to smash up the equipment. Whatever you find in there, wreck it utterly and completely, do you understand?' The two young men nodded.

'I thought these would be useful,' said Thomni. He produced a pair of long, heavy, iron-tipped staffs. Jamie took one and swung it appreciatively.

'Aye,' he said happily, 'that ought to do it.'

'It won't be any picnic,' warned the Doctor. 'The Intelligence has supernormal powers and it will use them all.'

'What kind of powers?' asked Victoria nervously.

'Well, it'll probably try to hypnotise you,' said the Doctor. 'Thomni, you teach her the "jewel in the lotus" prayer. That'll give her something to concentrate on…'

Their conference was interrupted by a chorus of shouts and screams from outside. Led by the Doctor, they rushed outside to see what was wrong.

In the courtyard the procession was ready to move off. But all the monks were gazing upwards, at the mountain. 'Look, Doctor,' called Sapan. 'The mountain is burning.'

The Doctor looked. The night was now so dark, and the flowing substance from the cave had now spread so far, that it could be clearly seen from the Monastery. It seemed as though the whole peak of the mountain was glowing and burning. And the glow was moving downwards.

The Doctor turned quickly to Sapan. 'There is even less time than I feared. You must lead your brethren away at once.'

Obediently the old lama began to give orders. The warrior monks marshalled the procession into line. They began to hand out torches for the steep climb down to the lower valley.

'Our brethren in the plains will give us shelter,' said Sapan. 'But I fear for you, Doctor. Will you not let our brave warriors stay and help you?'

'They are needed to guard you and your fellow lamas, Sapan,' replied the Doctor. 'Thomni is staying with me – he will be all the help I need.' The Doctor thought to himself that if the few of them couldn't succeed, a larger party would do no better. 'Go now, Sapan,' he said.

The little procession began to wind its way out of the courtyard and down the path. Standing by the doors, the Doctor and his companions watched the line of torches disappear into the darkness. Floating up to them came the sound of monks chanting the 'jewel in the lotus' prayer that Thomni had just taught Victoria.

'Om, mane, padme, hum.' The sound was curiously moving and beautiful.

At last the lights died away, the sounds faded and they were left alone. Victoria shivered. How strange and eerie to be the sole inhabitants of the Monastery! Except, that is, for whatever was lurking in the Sanctum.

'Will we shut the doors, Doctor?' asked Jamie.

The Doctor shrugged. 'No point, Jamie. We're fighting something inside as well as outside.' He glanced grimly up at the glowing, burning mountain for the last time, and led them back inside the Monastery.

As the little party disappeared inside the building, there was movement outside the doors. Yeti appeared from the darkness. Grouped in a semicircle, they stood waiting outside the gates.

Back in the Great Hall, the Doctor gave his companions a final briefing. 'As soon as we're in the control room, I'll tackle the Intelligence. Thomni and Jamie, move away the statue of Buddha at the end of the room. Get inside there and—'

'Aye, you've told us,' said Jamie. 'Smash the lot to bits!' He and Thomni picked up their massive, iron-tipped staffs. Jamie spun his, whistling it through the air.

'What about me?' asked Victoria. 'What do I do?'

'Nothing, I hope,' said the Doctor briskly. 'But you never know. Something may turn up.'

He hadn't the heart to tell Victoria she was only being included in the expedition because she would find it even more frightening to be left on her own. Moreover, win or lose, she'd be as safe with them as she would anywhere.

'Everybody ready?' asked the Doctor. 'Right, off we go.'

As they moved cautiously along the gloomy corridors, Jamie had a sudden thought.

'Hey, what happened to yon fellow Travers? I havena seen him.'

'Maybe he's deserted us,' suggested Victoria.

'I somehow doubt it,' said the Doctor. 'More likely he's gone off on some scheme of his own.'

'Well, he's no' here now, at any rate,' said Jamie. 'We'll just have to manage without him!' By the light of their flickering torches they crept forward along the echoing stone corridors towards the Inner Sanctum.

Travers, in fact, was very near. He was running full tilt down the last stretch of the path towards the Monastery. Far below him in the darkness he could see the torch-lit procession of the departing monks, and even hear their chanting.

As he came to the gates of the Monastery, Travers came to a sudden halt.

Standing grouped in a semicircle around the door was a group of Yeti – four of them. He wondered if they were activated or not. He picked up a big rock and rolled it towards them. Instantly all the Yeti swung round, alert to the movement. They were alive all right, thought Travers. Alive and waiting. There was nothing for it – he would have to wait, too.

Glancing back over his shoulder, he saw that the glowing mass was covering more and more of the mountain. It was moving nearer and nearer to the Monastery. Soon he would *have* to leave. Yet somehow, Travers felt that things were coming to a climax. He decided to wait as long as he could. Those Yeti were waiting for something, too.

The Doctor and his friends stopped in the corridor outside the Anteroom. 'Everyone remember what to do?' asked the Doctor. They all nodded. Jamie and Thomni took a firmer grip of their staves. 'All right,' said the Doctor. 'In we go!'

Their actual entrance into the Anteroom was something of an anti-climax. All was still and quiet. The prayer lamps were burning low and the place was shrouded in gloom and silence. Led by the Doctor, the little group moved forward.

The Doctor went up to the doors of the Inner Sanctum. He tried them, but they were fast closed. Suddenly, the voice of the Intelligence spoke to them, out of the air. There was a subtle change in its quality. It was harsher, colder, more inhuman, the traces of Padmasambvha's personality almost completely erased.

'Why are you here?' the voice said. 'Why do you not heed my warnings? You are stubborn, Doctor.'

'Who are you?' said the Doctor steadily. 'Or should I rather ask – what are you?'

A terrible mock-sweetness came into the alien voice. 'You know me well, Doctor. Am I not your old and treasured friend, Padmasambvha?'

'No!' said the Doctor. 'No, you are not. You have captured his spirit and abused his body. You have taken the mind and being of a good and great man, and corrupted and abused it. I ask again, who are you? Where do you come from?'

'I come from what you would call another dimension. I was exiled into yours, without physical substance; condemned to hover eternally between the stars. Then I made contact with the mind of Padmasambvha. He had journeyed further on the mental plane than any other of your kind. I tempted him, promised him knowledge and long life. Gradually I took him over, and made him my own. But I have rewarded him well.'

'You have enslaved him,' said the Doctor angrily. 'Now you withhold from him the one thing he craves – the boon of a natural death. You are evil. You are what men once called a demon!'

Jamie, Thomni and Victoria waited motionless behind the Doctor while this exchange was going on. 'It's all verra well standing here name-calling,' thought Jamie.

152

'How's he going to get the thing to open the door?'

Similar thoughts were passing through the Doctor's mind. His one hope was that the Intelligence had not realised that the power of Hypnotism was shared by the Doctor. So long as it was unaware of the extent and the value of the information he had drawn from the mind of Songtsen, they still had a fighting chance.

'You are unwise to anger me, Doctor,' said the voice. 'My purposes are beyond the understanding of such a puny brain as yours. And I have power. Much power...'

The Doctor made his voice deliberately contemptuous. 'You? Much power?'

Suddenly, one of the heavy bronze lamps flared up in a sheet of flame. It whizzed through the air like a cannon ball, missing the Doctor's head by inches, and crashed into the wall. The three others gasped in terror, but the Doctor didn't turn a hair.

'A little simple teleportation?' he said scornfully. 'Are you going to keep us here watching conjuring tricks? What next? Rabbits out of hats?'

'Aye, you're a cunning wee fellow, Doctor,' thought Jamie. 'Playing on its vanity. I hope it works. If we canna get into that Sanctum, we're done for.'

'Why don't you open those doors?' the Doctor said mockingly. 'Afraid to face us, are you?'

There was a moment of silence. Then slowly the doors swung open. The Doctor turned round to his companions.

'Anything may happen now. Anything at all. Trust

me. And, above all – don't panic.' Slowly he led them through the doors and into the Inner Sanctum.

Once inside, Jamie and Thomni looked in astonishment at the golden throne. The drapes were pulled now, obscuring it, but they could still see the little figure crouched over his table. A memory of some old fear passed through Victoria's mind, but she pushed it aside. She began to repeat the prayer that Thomni had taught her.

'Om, mane, padme, hum, om, mane, padme, hum.' She repeated the soothing words over and over.

Jamie looked at the little figure almost with pity. 'Och, is that all?' he thought. 'You could blow the wee fellow away with a sneeze.' Then, before he could move another step toward the dais, his whole body was caught by some terrifying invisible force.

He literally could not move a muscle. Thomni and Victoria were held in the same way. So too, it seemed, was the Doctor. Or was he? Slowly, with infinite effort, the Doctor managed to take first one step and then another. He directed the entire force of his will towards the little shrouded figure on the golden chair. The build-up of energy in the little room was overpowering. Suddenly, the blast of a mighty wind ripped through the room, sweeping away the draperies around the throne. Padmasambvha was revealed sitting bolt upright, eyes blazing with malignancy.

'Now!' yelled the Doctor. 'Now!'

Jamie felt the grip on him slacken. He saw that the

Doctor was standing in a half-crouch, one foot on the steps of the dais. His eyes were locked with those of the wizened figure on the throne. The effort required to do battle with the will of the Intelligence was distorting his face.

'Come on, Thomni,' yelled Jamie. 'Let's get to work.'

They ran to the golden statue of Buddha and swung it aside, following the instructions from Songtsen. The entrance to the hidden control room was revealed. But before they could enter, a high-pitched sound filled the room. Blinding lights flickered before their eyes. Jamie saw that the Doctor was sinking slowly to his knees. Then, with agonising slowness, the Doctor began to straighten up. His eyes fixed on those of the possessed Master, he took another step forward. A low ghastly moan filled the room as the Intelligence realised the strength of the mind that was opposing it.

'Come on, Thomni,' yelled Jamie. The two young men dashed into the secret control room. It was bare, and very small. All the walls were covered with an incredible tangle of equipment, of all ages and in all conditions – a mad, lunatic lash-up of electronics. At one end of the room a plain metal pyramid reposed on an altar. At the other end a glowing sphere, larger even than the ones which Jamie and Victoria had seen in the cave, caught their attention.

For a moment the two young men stood amazed. Then Jamie heard a strangled shout from the Doctor.

'Hurry, Jamie, hurry. Can't hold out much…'

Jamie raised his staff and smashed it down on a control panel. Thomni did the same. They worked frantically with great sweeping blows. Soon the entire control room was well on the way to being wrecked.

Outside in the Sanctum, Victoria watched as the Doctor waged his battle of wills with the Intelligence. She sensed a deadlock. Neither could afford the slightest distraction. Then to her horror she saw the withered hand of Padmasambvha creeping out towards the board.

'Look out, Doctor,' she called. 'He's going to bring the Yeti in.'

The Doctor redoubled his concentration, but he was unable to stop the movement of the hand. One by one, four of the Yeti models were placed on the map of the Monastery.

Outside the Monastery doors, Travers saw four of the Yeti move swiftly inside. Once they were under way, he started to follow them.

The Yeti seemed to move at a far greater speed than normal. As if impelled by some signal of great urgency, they rushed along the corridors, Travers trailing cautiously behind them.

Inside the Sanctum, the Doctor was still locked in struggle with the Intelligence. Like two wrestlers of exactly even strength, neither of them could move.

But the Doctor knew that the alien strength of the Intelligence would soon wear him down. And once he weakened, all would be over... They would all die.

Victoria watched helplessly. From inside the hidden control room came the sound of smashing equipment. Jamie and Thomni were going about their task with savage gusto. Then, from the corridor she heard the sound of roaring. The Yeti were coming!

'Victoria – get the models...' gasped the Doctor. 'Move them back...'

Victoria forced herself to go forward to the table. But the strength of the Intelligence's will was too much for her. Even locked in struggle with the Doctor, it stopped her from reaching the models.

'Resist it,' urged the Doctor. 'Say the prayer!'

Victoria tried. 'Om, mane, padme, hum. Om, mane, padme, hum...' But it was no use. She could *not* move her hand. And then it was too late. The Yeti burst into the room. As they lumbered towards him, the Doctor managed to yell, 'Jamie, Yeti... here...'

In the control room, Jamie and Thomni looked at each other.

'We have smashed all that controls them,' said Thomni. Jamie looked round.

'Aye, except this,' he said, and moved towards the sphere on the altar. Raising his staff above his head, he brought it smashing down on the sphere.

A Yeti, its arm drawn back to attack the Doctor, staggered back with a roar. There was an explosion from somewhere inside it, and it reeled away smoking, a hole blown in its chest. The control unit had exploded. The same happened to all its companions. They collapsed, shattered wrecks, on the floor.

The voice of the Intelligence said, 'You have destroyed my servants, but you have not destroyed me!'

Travers rushed into the room. Raising his rifle, he emptied the whole magazine into the figure on the throne.

It brushed its hand across its face as though swatting a fly, and then held out the hand. In it lay the spent bullets.

The Intelligence gave its terrible laugh. 'Oh foolish man,' it said. 'Did you not realise my power in the cave?'

The cave, thought the Doctor with the part of his mind that was still free. What did Travers tell me about the cave? Raising his voice, he yelled, 'Jamie, is there a pyramid in there?'

'Aye, there is that!' Jamie called back.

'Then smash it. Smash it now!'

In the control room Jamie and Thomni lashed with all their force at the pyramid. Suddenly it shattered into fragments as though made of glass.

Padmasambvha's body gave out a last terrible scream.

From somewhere outside came a series of rumbling explosions that shook the building. The cave in the mountain had exploded.

The body on the throne gave a sudden leap, falling from the throne. It landed across the little table, knocking it to the ground. With a final convulsive twitch, the

Intelligence left it.

The Doctor lifted the shrivelled body in his arms. Worn out by years of slavery, it was almost weightless. Suddenly Padmasambvha's eyes opened. He saw the Doctor looking down at him, and smiled.

Victoria realised that, for the first time, they were seeing the real Padmasambvha, free of the Intelligence. When he spoke, his voice was warm and gentle, the voice of a wise old man.

'At last, I shall have peace… I waited so long, Doctor. I knew you would come, and save me from myself…'

The old man's head fell back.

'Goodbye, old friend,' said the Doctor, and lowered the frail body to the ground. Jamie and Thomni emerged from the control room.

'It worked,' said the Doctor. 'The Intelligence is destroyed. My old friend Padmasambvha can rest at last.'

They all walked slowly from the Sanctum, and made their way back to the courtyard.

'Look,' said Travers, and pointed. They all looked up. The glow had gone from the mountain. The explosion in the cave had destroyed the physical being of the Intelligence.

'Yes,' said the Doctor. 'It's really over at last.' He yawned and stretched.

'You know, I think I could do with some sleep.'

12

The Abominable Snowman

Next morning, as the Doctor, Jamie, Victoria and Travers came out into the courtyard, they were greeted by a deafening clang. Thomni was solemnly banging an enormous gong. 'What on earth are you doing?' asked Victoria, her hands over her ears.

'It is the hour for morning prayer, Miss Victoria,' explained Thomni.

Victoria frowned. 'But there's no one here but you.'

'All the more reason that I should strictly observe the rituals, until my brothers return,' said Thomni. 'They will hear the gong and know that all is well.'

'Time we all said goodbye, I'm afraid,' said the Doctor.

Thomni looked disappointed. 'Can you not stay until my brethren return? They will wish to thank you.'

'I'm afraid not,' said the Doctor hastily. 'You see, I'm worried about my equipment. It might have been damaged when the top of the mountain exploded.'

Thomni looked at the mountain. It was now quite a different shape at the top, part of the upper peak having been blown away. 'Very well then, Doctor. Goodbye and thank you again.' After more farewells, Travers said, 'I'll see you safely up the mountain, Doctor!'

Nothing they could say would dissuade him, and they all set off up the mountain path together. Looking back, they could see that once again the doors of Detsen Monastery stood wide and welcoming. Victoria just caught a fleeting glimpse of Thomni setting off for prayers in a one-man procession. She smiled. He really had been very nice. But very solemn.

Jamie came up close to the Doctor and whispered, 'You're not really worried about the TARDIS, are you, Doctor?'

The Doctor shook his head. 'The TARDIS is indestructible, Jamie, you know that. No, I just thought it was time we were leaving.'

Jamie indicated Travers, who was happily marching on ahead.

'What about him, Doctor? The TARDIS will be a bit of a shock to him.'

'I know,' said the Doctor. 'That's been worrying me rather. But he won't take any hints!'

There came a shout from Travers. He had stopped, and was waving to them. 'Look at this!' The shattered body of a Yeti lay across the path. 'Its chest unit must have exploded at the same time as those in the Sanctum,' said Jamie.

'Wonderful machines, those,' said the Doctor. 'Almost a shame to have destroyed them. Something for you to take back from your expedition at any rate, Mr Travers.'

Travers sighed. 'They'd only say it was a fake. If they

won't believe in the real Yeti, they certainly wouldn't credit what's happened here.'

Walking round the shattered robot, they went on. 'You really needn't trouble to come with us any further, Mr Travers,' said the Doctor.

'Ay, that's right,' agreed Jamie eagerly. 'No doubt you'll want to be off hunting your beasties!'

'I'm thinking of giving all that up,' said Travers gloomily. 'I'm only getting myself laughed at. Wretched thing's probably only a legend anyway.'

'Don't give up, whatever you do,' urged the Doctor. 'It's a splendid thing to have a dream... even if it does turn out to be a legend.'

'Maybe,' said Travers, but he didn't sound convinced. 'Let's get on,' he suggested. 'I'm looking forward to seeing this camp of yours.'

The Doctor and his companions exchanged glances, and they all walked on. The journey became more difficult now as they climbed higher. The explosion at the cave had thrown down rocks and boulders which covered the path, and they had to clamber over and round them. 'Much further, is it?' puffed Travers.

The Doctor shook his head resignedly. 'Not far. Once we get through that clump of boulders we'll be there.'

A few minutes later, Travers was staring in utter amazement at the old blue police box perched incongruously on a mountain ledge. 'My word,' he said. 'What the blazes is that doing here?'

The Doctor cleared his throat. 'Well, as a matter of

fact, Mr Travers,' he began. There came a sudden scream from Victoria. 'Look – another Yeti. It's moving.'

'That's impossible!' said the Doctor. They all looked where she was pointing. Not far away, behind some boulders, a creature was peering shyly at them.

'It's different!' said Victoria. 'Not like the others at all!' And so it was. It was taller and less bulky. The fur was longer and silkier, and had a more reddish tint. Above all, the face was different, rather like that of a lemur, with dark, soft eyes. Travers was looking at it entranced. 'Don't you see?' he said. 'It's a Yeti. It's a real Yeti, not some wretched robot. I've found it. I've found it at last!'

Travers began stumbling towards the Yeti, across the mountain slope. For a moment the creature watched him approach. Then it gave a curiously high-pitched squeal of fright and disappeared behind a boulder. Travers broke into a run, and soon he too had disappeared from view.

'I rather think this is our opportunity,' said the Doctor. 'No need to worry about Mr Travers' reaction to the TARDIS. By now he's forgotten its existence.'

'Do you think he'll catch his Yeti, Doctor?' asked Victoria.

'That doesn't really matter,' said the Doctor gently. 'The important thing is, he's found his dream again.'

Jamie shivered. 'Let's be away then, Doctor,' he said. 'It's no' a bad place, this Tibet of yours, but it's awful chilly. Next time you want to visit some old friends, can you no' make it somewhere warmer?'

'Honestly, Jamie, you're always grumbling,' said

Victoria. 'Anyway, you know the Doctor's got no idea where the TARDIS will finish up next.'

'That's most unfair, Victoria,' protested the Doctor. 'There may be the occasional navigational error, but basically I am fully in control – well, more or less.'

Wrangling amiably the three companions walked across the snow and disappeared inside the TARDIS. After a moment, a strange groaning noise echoed through the mountain air, and the old blue police box shimmered and vanished. The Doctor and his friends were off on their next adventure.

About the Authors

Terrance Dicks

Born in East Ham in London in 1935, Terrance Dicks worked in the advertising industry after leaving university before moving into television as a writer. He worked together with Malcolm Hulke on scripts for *The Avengers* as well as other series before becoming Assistant and later full Script Editor of *Doctor Who* from 1968.

Working closely with friend and series Producer Barry Letts, Dicks worked on the entirety of the Third Doctor Jon Pertwee's era of the programme, and returned as a writer – scripting Tom Baker's first story as the Fourth Doctor: 'Robot'. He left *Doctor Who* to work as first Script Editor and then Producer on the BBC's prestigious Classic Serials, and to pursue his writing career on screen and in print. His later scriptwriting credits on *Doctor Who* included the twentieth-anniversary story 'The Five Doctors'.

Terrance Dicks novelised many of the original *Doctor Who* stories for Target, and discovered a liking and talent for prose fiction. He has written extensively for children, creating such memorable series and characters as T.R. Bear and the Baker Street Irregulars, as well as continuing to write original *Doctor Who* novels for BBC Books.

Mervyn Haisman and Henry Lincoln

Mervyn Haisman and Henry Lincoln worked, together and separately, on scripts for various TV series in the 1960s, including *Doctor Finlay's Casebook*, *Emergency Ward 10* and *Doctor Who*. They also wrote the script for the 1968 horror film *Curse of the Crimson Altar*.

Two of their *Doctor Who* scripts featured the Yeti – servants of an alien intelligence – which proved very popular and memorable. The second of these stories, 'The Web of Fear', also introduced the character of Colonel Lethbridge-Stewart who – promoted to Brigadier – became a regular character when the Third Doctor worked with UNIT during the early 1970s. Their third script together, 'The Dominators', credited to the pseudonymous Norman Ashby, introduced the Quarks.

Haisman, who had previously been an actor, and managed a theatre company, continued to write television during the 1970s and 1980s. He died in October 2010, aged 82.

Lincoln, who had also been an actor under his real name of Henry Soskin, developed a fascination with the mysteries surrounding the French village of Rennes-le-Château and scripted and presented a series of documentaries about it for the BBC in the 1970s. He co-authored the book *The Holy Blood and the Holy Grail*, much of which was based on his own research and ideas from which were incorporated into Dan Brown's phenomenally successful novel *The Da Vinci Code*. Lincoln now lives and works in Rennes-le-Château.

The first full year of *Doctor Who* publishing from Target began and ended with books written by Terrance Dicks. Seven novelisations came out in 1974, beginning with *Doctor Who and the Auton Invasion* in January and culminating, in November, with *Doctor Who and the Abominable Snowmen*. Dicks's third contribution was his first featuring a past Doctor; although the range had been launched the previous year with reprints of three First Doctor adventures, the bulk of the new paperbacks featured Jon Pertwee's Third Doctor. On television, the Fourth Doctor, Tom Baker, was about to make his debut, and *Doctor Who and the Abominable Snowmen* was the first of just six Second Doctor novels released in the 1970s.

Written by Mervyn Haisman and Henry Lincoln, 'The Abominable Snowmen' was originally broadcast in six 25-minute episodes from 30 September to 4 November 1967, the second serial in *Doctor Who*'s fifth season. Terrance Dicks's novelisation was published by Universal-Tandem Publishing as a Target paperback on 21 November 1974. The cover illustration was by Chris Achilleos, the artist responsible for the twenty-eight Target covers during the first four years of the range. Interior drawings (used in this edition) were by Alan Willow, who had already illustrated *Doctor Who and the Daemons* and *Doctor Who and the Sea Devils*; he subsequently illustrated *Doctor Who and the Curse of Peladon*, *Doctor Who and the Cybermen*, *Doctor Who and the Terror of the Autons* and *Doctor Who and the Green Death*.

This new edition re-presents that 1974 version. While a few minor errors or inconsistencies have been corrected, no attempt has been made to update or modernise the text – this is *Doctor Who and the Abominable Snowmen* as originally written and published.

This means that the novel retains certain stylistic and editorial practices that were current in 1974 but which have since adapted or changed. Most obviously, measurements are given in the then-standard imperial system of weights and measures: a yard is equivalent to 0.9144 metres; three feet make a yard, and a foot is 30 centimetres; twelve inches make a foot, and an inch is 25.4 millimetres.

When adapting scripts for novelisation, Terrance Dicks often took the opportunity to expand on what had been seen on screen. Extended and invented scenes are a regular feature of Terrance Dicks's mid-1970s *Doctor Who* novelisations, as seen in *Doctor Who and the Auton Invasion* and *Doctor Who and the Day of the Daleks*. (The latter, for example, includes a televised scene in which the Third Doctor and his assistant Jo meet future versions of themselves, then follows it up with an untelevised scene in which those future versions encounter their earlier selves.) 'The Abominable Snowmen' offers fewer opportunities for this sort of invention, and these are largely confined to the character of Edward Travers. Episode 1's opening scene lasted less than a minute, with Travers woken by the dying screams of his colleague 'John'. The novel's first couple of pages greatly extend this, giving John a surname (Mackay) and Edward Travers a back story. Travers' troubled dreams of the Royal Geographical Society and its members' cynical response to his theories help explain both his fanatical zeal and his later unhinged state. And Jamie's scheme to capture a Yeti here receives the Doctor's complete backing and trust, in contrast with its humorously panicked reception in the second episode on television.

In other respects, the novel presents a very faithful retelling of the TV story – if snowier (the serial was filmed in the distinctly un-snowy hills of North Wales). Perhaps the most significant difference between the two versions is in the names of the various monks of the Det-sen monastery. Haisman and Lincoln had based these on those of authentic and noteworthy figures from Tibetan Buddhist history: Songtsän Gampo founded the Tibetan empire in the seventh century; Thonmi Sambhota was the inventor of Tibetan script at the behest of Songtsän Gampo; Padmasambhava was an eighth-century sage guru who took Vajrayana Buddhism to Tibet; in the ninth century, Tri Ralpacen was the forty-first King of Tibet, another important figure in the progress of Buddhism;

Buton Rinchen Drub was a fourteenth-century Tibetan abbott. When Terrance Dicks was commissioned to novelise 'The Abominable Snowman', *Doctor Who*'s producer was Barry Letts. Letts was uncomfortable with this use of genuine names and concerned that it might cause inadvertent offence. He advised Dicks to make small changes to them. Consequently, TV's Abbot Songsten becomes Abbot Songtsen, Thonmi becomes Thomni, Padmasambhava becomes Padmasambvha, Ralpachan becomes Rapalchan… Only Rinchen and Khrisong remain unchanged.

Doctor Who and the Abominable Snowman also has a few examples of one of the many things Terrance Dicks has influenced or devised for the *Doctor Who* universe. On television, Jon Pertwee, Patrick Troughton and, especially, William Hartnell portray the Doctor as a rather *human* alien – he is subject to many of the limitations and frailties that most Earthlings face. A consistent feature of Dicks's novelisations, though, is a continuing series of hints that the Doctor's unprepossessing appearance masks something more powerful. 'Although the Doctor was small in stature, he seemed to have limitless resources of energy and strength,' the book tells us. 'Despite his modest size, the Doctor could exert amazing strength when he needed to.' It could only be a matter of time before the Doctor would be unveiled as one of the few two-armed beings in the universe to have mastered the martial art of Venusian Aikido…

Here are details of other exciting Doctor Who *titles from BBC Books:*

DOCTOR WHO AND THE DALEKS
David Whitaker   £4.99
ISBN 978 1 849 90195 6   **A First Doctor adventure**

With a new introduction by **NEIL GAIMAN**

*'The voice was all on one level, without any expression at all,
a dull monotone that still managed to convey a terrible sense
of evil...'*

The mysterious Doctor and his granddaughter Susan
are joined by unwilling adventurers Ian Chesterton and
Barbara Wright in an epic struggle for survival on an alien
planet.

In a vast metal city they discover the survivors of a
terrible nuclear war – the Daleks. Held captive in the
deepest levels of the city, can the Doctor and his new
companions stop the Daleks' plan to totally exterminate
their mortal enemies, the peace-loving Thals? More
importantly, even if they can escape from the Daleks, will
Ian and Barbara ever see their home planet Earth again?

This novel is based on the second Doctor Who *story, which
was originally broadcast from 21 December 1963 to 1
February 1964. This was the first ever* Doctor Who *novel,
first published in 1964.*

DOCTOR WHO AND THE CRUSADERS
David Whitaker   £4.99
ISBN 978 1 849 90190 1   **A First Doctor adventure**

With a new introduction by **CHARLIE HIGSON**

'I admire bravery, sir. And bravery and courage are clearly in you in full measure. Unfortunately, you have no brains at all. I despise fools.'

Arriving in the Holy Land in the middle of the Third Crusade, the Doctor and his companions run straight into trouble. The Doctor and Vicki befriend Richard the Lionheart, but must survive the cut-throat politics of the English court. Even with the king on their side, they find they have made powerful enemies.

Looking for Barbara, Ian is ambushed – staked out in the sand and daubed with honey so that the ants will eat him. With Ian unable to help, Barbara is captured by the cruel warlord El Akir. Even if Ian escapes and rescues her, will they ever see the Doctor, Vicki and the TARDIS again?

This novel is based on a Doctor Who *story which was originally broadcast from 27 March to 17 April 1965, featuring the First Doctor as played by William Hartnell, and his companions Ian, Barbara and Vicki.*

DOCTOR WHO AND THE CYBERMEN
Gerry Davis   £4.99
ISBN 978 1 849 90191 8   **A Second Doctor adventure**

With a new introduction by **GARETH ROBERTS**

*'There are some corners of the universe which have bred the
most terrible things. Things which are against everything we
have ever believed in. They must be fought. To the death.'*

In 2070, the Earth's weather is controlled from a base on
the moon. But when the Doctor and his friends arrive, all
is not well. They discover unexplained drops of air pressure,
minor problems with the weather control systems, and an
outbreak of a mysterious plague.

With Jamie injured, and members of the crew going
missing, the Doctor realises that the moonbase is under
attack. Some malevolent force is infecting the crew and
sabotaging the systems as a prelude to an invasion of
Earth. And the Doctor thinks he knows who is behind it:
the Cybermen.

*This novel is based on 'The Moonbase', a Doctor Who story
which was originally broadcast from 11 February to 4 March
1967, featuring the Second Doctor as played by Patrick
Troughton, and his companions Polly, Ben and Jamie.*

DOCTOR WHO AND THE AUTON INVASION
Terrance Dicks   £4.99
ISBN 978 1 849 90193 2   **A Third Doctor adventure**

With a new introduction by **RUSSELL T DAVIES**

'Here at UNIT we deal with the odd – the unexplained. We're prepared to tackle anything on Earth. Or even from beyond the Earth, if necessary.'

Put on trial by the Time Lords, and found guilty of interfering in the affairs of other worlds, the Doctor is exiled to Earth in the 20th century, his appearance once again changed. His arrival coincides with a meteorite shower. But these are no ordinary meteorites.

The Nestene Consciousness has begun its first attempt to invade Earth using killer Autons and deadly shop window dummies. Only the Doctor and UNIT can stop the attack. But the Doctor is recovering in hospital, and his old friend the Brigadier doesn't even recognise him. Can the Doctor recover and win UNIT's trust before the invasion begins?

This novel is based on 'Spearhead from Space', a Doctor Who story which was originally broadcast from 3 to 24 January 1970, featuring the Third Doctor as played by Jon Pertwee, with his companion Liz Shaw and the UNIT organisation commanded by Brigadier Lethbridge-Stewart.

DOCTOR WHO AND THE CAVE MONSTERS
Malcolm Hulke   £4.99
ISBN 978 1 849 90194 9   **A Third Doctor adventure**

With a new introduction by **TERRANCE DICKS**

'Okdel looked across the valley to see the tip of the sun as it sank below the horizon. It was the last time he was to see the sun for a hundred million years.'

UNIT are called in to investigate security at a secret research centre buried under Wenley Moor. Unknown to the Doctor and his colleagues, the work at the centre has woken a group of Silurians – intelligent reptiles that used to be the dominant life form on Earth in prehistoric times.

Now they have woken, the Silurians are appalled to find 'their' planet populated by upstart apes. The Doctor hopes to negotiate a peace deal, but there are those on both sides who cannot bear the thought of humans and Silurians living together. As UNIT soldiers enters the cave systems, and the Silurians unleash a deadly plague that could wipe out the human race, the battle for planet Earth begins.

This novel is based on 'The Silurians', a Doctor Who story which was originally broadcast from 31 January to 14 March 1970, featuring the Third Doctor as played by Jon Pertwee, with his companion Liz Shaw and the UNIT organisation commanded by Brigadier Lethbridge-Stewart.

BBC

NEW RELEASES

DOCTOR WHO

New classic

DOCTOR WHO

releases from

AudioGO